Read all the books about Madison Finn!

Coming Soon!

Don't miss the Super Edition

From the Files of

Madison Finn

Three's a Crowd

By Laura Dower

HYPERION
New York

Text copyright © 2004 by Laura Dower

From the Files of Madison Finn and the Volo colophon are trademarks of Disney Enterprises, Inc.
Volo® is a registered trademark of Disney Enterprises, Inc.

Printed in the United States of America

First Edition
5 7 9 10 8 6 4

The main body of text of this book is set in 13-point Frutiger Roman.

ISBN 0-7868-0986-8

Visit www.hyperionbooksforchildren.com

For Rich, Myles, and Olivia,
my "crowd" of three

Chapter 1

As Madison Finn glared at the writing on the blackboard in Mr. Gibbons's classroom, the words blurred together. Her eyes watered, so she reached into her orange bag for a tissue.

> Today's Mental Floss
> If an international airliner crashed exactly
> on the U.S.–Mexican border, where would
> authorities be required to bury the survivors?

Madison blinked. The answer didn't come easily. And now her nose was leaking. Why wasn't the cold pill Mom had given her that morning at breakfast working? Forget the cold pill. Why wasn't her *brain* working?

"Mr. Gibbons always asks such BOGUS stuff," Egg Diaz whispered to Madison. Egg was one of Madison's best guy friends. He was a whiz at video games, computers, *and* complaining.

"Mental floss? Like my brain isn't tired enough," sniffed Fiona Waters, one of Madison's best girl-friends. Her nose was running, too.

"Shhhhh!" Madison said. She didn't want Mr. Gibbons to catch them talking when they should all have been working out the answer.

Unbeknownst to her pals, Madison secretly loved all the brain twisters and obscure homework assignments Mr. Gibbons offered in his class. They made her think differently. She liked that. Unfortunately, that day's "floss" had all three friends super stumped. They would have to wait until the end of class for an answer. The three pulled out their copies of *The Outsiders* for class discussion.

"Before we get started, I have a special assignment for you," Mr. Gibbons announced to the room with a wink. "It's a creative research project that the entire seventh grade will be working on. . . ."

"Oh, no," a boy in the back of the room groaned. "Isn't it early in the year for a research project?"

Mr. Gibbons chuckled. "Quite the contrary, Mark," he said, shuffling the stack. "Early on is a perfect time to get serious about your work. Don't you all think so?"

Now *everyone* in the room groaned.

Row by row, Mr. Gibbons passed out sets of stapled yellow pages. On the top page, Madison read the bold, blue headline, "Cross-Curricular Seventh Grade Web Page Project." She glanced over at Egg with a half grin. Together, she, Egg, and their other friend Drew Maxwell, worked on the school Web site together. Maybe this assignment wouldn't be so awful after all. . . .

"As you can see," Mr. Gibbons continued. "This isn't really an English assignment. It covers *all* subjects. The twist is that you'll be doing your paper online and with a team of students. Your other seventh grade teachers will be discussing more with you today."

Madison's eyes scanned the page.

```
Suggested Web page Topics:

• Egyptians and the pyramids
• UFO sightings: real or hoax?
• Sinking of the Titanic
• The origins of baseball and how
  the game has changed
• Saving the Alaskan Wildlife Refuge
• Magic and optical illusions
• Ben Franklin's inventions


Be creative. But think smart. No
Web essays on extreme sports, serial
killers, video games, or biographies
```

of current celebrities, rap stars, or sports stars. All topics must be approved first.

Although it seemed like an interesting project, Madison found herself staring into space, or at least into the space on the linoleum floor between the two desks in front of her. It was getting harder and harder to think about work—or anything else—when her ears felt this hot.

"Maddie?" Fiona sniffled again. "You don't look so good."

"Huh?" Madison grunted, turning around to face her friend. She coughed. "Yeah. I don't feel so good."

"Did you see Aimee this morning?" Fiona asked. "She isn't feeling so good, either."

Aimee Gillespie was Madison's and Fiona's other best friend.

"Ladies?" Mr. Gibbons said as he came and stood between them. "Can I help you with something? Do you have questions about the handout?"

Fiona let out a loud cough. "Um . . . not exactly."

"Gee, that cough doesn't sound too good," Mr. Gibbons commented.

"I'm sort of sick," Fiona admitted.

"There are a lot of sick kids in school today," Mr. Gibbons mused.

"I know. Madison is sick, too," Fiona added.

Right on cue, Madison wiped her eyes and nose with wadded-up tissue.

"Oh, I get it," Mr. Gibbons said with a smile. He scratched his head and pointed to the classroom door. "Maybe you two should take a walk . . . to the nurse."

Fiona let out a satisfied squeak as Mr. Gibbons walked back to his desk to fill out a hall pass.

"You're good, Fiona," Madison said under her breath. She reached down for her orange bag with another loud sniffle.

"You always get to escape," Egg said. "Typical."

"Oh, Egg," Fiona said, holding back more sniffles. She cocked her head to the side and laughed a little. Even sick, Fiona found ways to flirt with Egg. They'd been "dating" since seventh grade started. Of course their dates mostly consisted of group trips to Freeze Palace, the movies, and the library, but they were still happy to be called a couple.

No one in class seemed to pay much attention to Fiona or Madison as they headed for the door. Everyone else was too busy reading and talking about the new Web page project.

"Look over that work sheet, you hear?" Mr. Gibbons told Fiona and Madison as he handed them the hall pass. "And read chapters eight and nine in *The Outsiders*. I hope you're back in class tomorrow."

"Um . . . Mr. Gibbons?" Madison asked before walking out. "What was today's floss?" Normally,

Mr. Gibbons gave kids the answer at the end of class. Madison couldn't leave without finding out.

"Ahhh. The floss! Today's was a really tricky question," he said quietly, so that no one else in the room would hear. "Read it carefully again, Madison. Think. Why would anyone bury *survivors*?"

"Duh!" Madison said groggily. "That's a good one."

"How do you think this stuff up?" Fiona asked with a cough.

Mr. Gibbons shook his head. "Get thyselves to the nurse's office, young ladies, before we all catch your bugs, okay?"

Madison slung her bag over her shoulder and followed Fiona to the staircase. Together they headed to Nurse Shim's office, otherwise known as The Dungeon, because it was located in the basement at school. Sometimes kids called Nurse Shim the Dungeon Keeper. Entering her dark office was like entering a prison with checkpoints and sign-up sheets and NO TALKING signs posted everywhere. She was the ogress of Far Hills Junior High, and everyone knew better than to cross her.

"Hall passes, pah-lease!" Nurse Shim cried as soon as Fiona and Madison entered the office.

At the front of the office sat a very large desk, chairs, and a giant, fluorescent floor lamp with a lampshade like a turban. In the back were a few musty-smelling cots. Along the side walls stood cabinets half filled with bandages, tissues, cotton balls, and other first-aid items. The school had used to store aspirin and other medicines, but then the rules had changed. Medication was no longer distributed on the premises.

Madison and Fiona quickly produced their passes and sat down in a couple of the metal chairs in front of Nurse Shim's desk. Since they both complained of fever and chills, each girl was given a thermometer to check her temperature.

"One hundred and one degrees," Nurse Shim said as she read Fiona's thermometer. Madison's was close to 102. "I guess we're sending you gals home."

Nurse Shim picked up her telephone. "What's your mom's number?" She asked Fiona first. Fiona wheezed a little as she repeated the number and watched Nurse Shim dial.

"Hey! Fiona! Maddie! What are you guys doing here?" a voice called out from the doorway.

Madison and Fiona whirled around to see Aimee standing there. She had her backpack and coat in her arms.

Nurse Shim grabbed Aimee's pass, too. "Sit," she barked.

Aimee rolled her eyes and sneezed. "I feel so-o-o gross," she mumbled to her friends, collapsing into a chair. "Why are you here?"

"This so weird," Madison said. "We're all sick at the same time. What are the odds of that?"

"I'd rather be anywhere but here." Aimee sneezed again.

"What a weird coincidence. Like fate or something. Don'tcha think?" Fiona said, rubbing her nose.

"Excuse me, ladies," Nurse Shim interrupted with a scowl. "Miss Waters, I spoke to your father and he will be coming to school to get you. Now, what about you, Miss Finn? Whom should I call?"

"My mom is in a work meeting," Madison said. "And I don't know where the meeting is."

Madison didn't want to admit that she'd left a slip of paper with all of Mom's contact information on the kitchen counter at home.

Whoops.

"What about your father?" Nurse Shim asked.

"He's away on business," Madison said.

"Can't you call your mom on her cell phone?" Fiona asked.

Madison shook her head. "She doesn't have it. It broke last week."

Nurse Shim tapped her fingers on her big steel desk. "Without a parent's consent, you cannot leave the school," she said, clucking her tongue.

"I have an idea," Aimee cut in. "Call your dad on *his* cell and then call my mom. I know he'll give permission for her to come get us both."

Much to Madison's relief, Aimee's idea was a slam dunk. Nurse Shim got the permission she needed from Madison's dad, and Mrs. Gillespie agreed to pick up both Aimee and Madison. She told them she would meet the girls in front of the school in fifteen minutes.

Aimee, Fiona, and Madison gathered their belongings and headed toward the front lobby as Nurse Shim waved them on with a grunt. Two other kids with sniffles and hall passes were waiting for her immediate attention.

As the girls made their way to the front lobby, the bell rang for the changing of classes. Kids poured into the hallway, rushing to lockers and classrooms.

"Maddie! Fiona! Aim! Over here!" a voice called out. It was Lindsay, their other BFF, heading back to her own locker. "Where have you been?" Lindsay asked, juggling a stack of books in her hands. Lindsay was usually heading to or coming from the school library and media center.

In response, Madison, Fiona, and Aimee coughed at the same time.

"Are you three sick?" Lindsay asked.

Madison rubbed her nose. "Don't I look like Rudolph?" she said. "My nose feels redder than red."

"Wow. You should go to the nurse," Lindsay suggested.

"We just left. She sent us home," Fiona said.

"We're on our way to the lobby. . . ." Aimee said.

9

"How did you all get sick at the same time?" Lindsay asked.

Madison shrugged. "Lucky, I guess."

Brrrrrrrring.

"That's the bell. I'm late. Somebody call me later!" Lindsay said, dashing off to her next class.

As they turned another corner, Madison nearly collided with Ivy Daly, her archenemy, otherwise known as Poison Ivy.

"Excuse ME!" Ivy cried when Madison nearly knocked her over. "What is your problem? Oh, wait! I know what your problem is. . . ."

Madison let out a loud, hacking cough.

"Ewwwww!" Ivy said, taking a step back. "Get away from me. I don't want your germs. Disgusting."

"Gee, thanks," Madison said as the enemy turned and retreated to her own locker. Madison felt clammier than clammy. There was no question about it: she had to get out of school—now.

"She's the one who's disgusting," Aimee scoffed. "Finnster!"

Hart Jones came up behind Madison and thwacked her on the back. She turned, stunned. Madison didn't want Hart to see her that way, looking like death warmed over.

"Hey, Hart," Madison mumbled, staring down at the floor. Her head was really spinning now—and it wasn't just because of the fever. Since the beginning of junior high, she'd had a huge crush on Hart.

Lately the burning question was: did he feel the same way?

"Where are you headed?" Hart asked when he spied her coat and orange book bag.

"Headed? Oh. Home." Madison coughed again. "You?" The only words she produced were monosyllables. She sounded like a computer recording.

"Me? I'm off to second period. . . ." Hart said. He stared down at his sneakers and bobbed from side to side. "Hey, did you get that research-paper assignment in first period?"

Before she could answer, Madison felt a sneeze coming on. "Aaah . . . aaah . . ."

She quickly bit her tongue. It was a trick Gramma Helen had taught her: if you bit the very tip of your tongue you could short-circuit sneezes, itches, and all kinds of twitches.

Unfortunately, it didn't work this time.

"Aaah . . . CHOOOOOOOO!"

Hart took a slow step backward and glanced down at his sweater. Madison was afraid to look.

From down the hall, Chet Waters, Fiona's twin brother, came running. "Hart!" he cried. "Wait up!"

"Here comes bigmouth," Fiona groaned. "We better split. I can't deal with Chet right now."

"Yeah, let's go," Aimee said, tugging on Madison's sleeve. "My mom will be waiting downstairs for us."

Madison smiled. Hart smiled, too. He didn't seem

fazed at all by the sweater sneezing incident. In fact, he looked right into Madison's eyes, like he was staring *through* her.

"Hope you feel better soon," Hart said.

As they walked away, Aimee grabbed Madison around the waist and leaned in close. "Way to flirt, Maddie," she whispered.

Madison gasped. "What?" she said. "I wasn't flirting."

"Well, so what? *He* was," Aimee said, pinching Madison's arm.

Fiona laughed. "Definitely," she said, pinching Madison's other arm.

Madison had kept her crush a secret for a long time, but now her friends knew everything. Lindsay knew, too. And it was better that way. It was too hard to keep big secrets from best friends. Plus, like Aimee had said, it was kinda obvious.

In the school lobby, the three BFFs sat together on a wooden bench, waiting for their parents and comparing aches and pains.

Aimee pulled out the same yellow research-paper sheet that Madison and Fiona had gotten in Mr. Gibbons's class and waved it in the air. "What do you think about this project?" she asked her friends.

"Way too hard," Fiona chimed in. "On top of all our other homework, too!"

"Could be fun though, especially since it's on the Web," Madison said.

"You think everything about the Web is fun," Aimee teased. She blew her nose loudly.

Madison rolled her eyes.

"But what's with the 'team' thing?" Fiona asked aloud.

"Knowing my luck, I'll get teamed with Poison Ivy. That would be the worst," Madison said.

"I thought we could pick our own teams," Aimee said.

"Really?" Madison said.

"If that's true, then why don't *we* do the project together?" Fiona said.

Madison's mind started spinning in a whole new direction.

"You mean, me, you, and Aim as a team?" Madison asked. "Cool."

"Unless you'd rather team up with *Hart*. . . ." Aimee said.

Fiona laughed so hard she started to cough.

"Very funny, you two," Madison moaned. She wiped her nose.

"There's Mom!" Aimee shouted, pointing across the school parking lot. Pulling in directly behind the Gillespie minivan was Fiona's dad, driving their family car. He honked.

"When can we talk more about the project?" Fiona asked as she headed toward her dad's car.

"Just E me later," Aimee suggested.

"And E . . . aaah . . . CHOOOOO!" Madison

sneezed again. "E me, too," she said, eyes watering.

Aimee held the door open for Madison. Both girls waved good-bye to Fiona.

Warm and breezy September air blew outside the school building. Of course, Madison had chills and hot sweats at the same time, so she wasn't really sure what the real temperature was.

Besides, Madison had other things on her mind.

Like Hart.

And all signs seemed to indicate that Hart had Madison on *his* mind, too.

Chapter 2

 Sick

Rude Awakening: Here's a new way to survive seventh grade: Just flu it.

After leaving school early today, I drove with Aimee over to her house. Mrs. Gillespie made this tofu broth soup thing that made me want to puke. How am I supposed to eat mystery food when I have chills and a fever? I don't know how Aim eats that stuff. It had green strands in it called seaweed kelp. HELP!

Anyway, Mom came home late, around 2, from her meeting. She picked me up in the car even though we're only a few houses down the block. Mom was so worried that she

took me over to Dr. Pinkerton's office
pronto. Naturally, we had to wait an hour
before they called me. There were so many
people in there hacking and snorting and
UGH. At least I cover my mouth when I hack.
Ha-ha.

The news is not good. Apparently, I have
acute bronchitis. That's what the doctor
called it. At first I thought he was
telling me *I* was cute LOL but of course I
just heard him wrong. Bronchitis means I
have too much congestion in my chest and an
inflammation of my bronchial tubes and my
cough will get worse this week before it
gets better. And oh yeah, my throat hurts.
A LOT. Lucky for me, Mrs. Gillespie gave me
homeopathic mints called Flu-Ease that help
because they have eucalyptus, so whenever I
swallow, my throat feels icy instead of
stinging hot.

Mom couldn't believe that Aim, Fiona,
and I all got sick at the same time. But
it makes perfect sense to me. Best friends
stick together, right? Or is that best
friends SICK together?

I feel like my head is going to explode.
I'd better go ask Mom for a cup of herbal
tea with extra honey. It's funny how much I
love to drink that when I'm sick even
though I never drink it any other time.

"Maddie," Mom appeared at Madison's bedroom
door with mug in hand. "I made you something. . . ."

16

Madison sniffed the air. She smelled honey. Mom was a mind reader.

Madison quickly hit SAVE and shut down her computer. Behind Mom, Madison's dog, Phin, darted into the room, too, with a squeaky, rubber, toy chicken in his jaws.

"Roooooooowf!" Phin dropped the chicken and scratched at the bedcovers. He wanted to play.

Mom pulled back on his collar. "No, Phinnie," she said sternly. "No, no, no!"

"Mom?" Madison didn't know why her mom was getting so angry. "Are you okay?" she asked.

Mom sat on the corner of the bed. "Aw, I'm fine, Maddie," she stammered. "I just . . . I just . . . have a lot on my mind, that's all. We have a major deadline next week . . . and this morning's meeting didn't go as well as I'd hoped . . . and . . ."

"Oh," Madison said, taking a sip of her tea.

"And I was supposed to have a second round of meetings early this evening, but now . . . we spent all that time at the doctor's office. . . . I can't possibly make it now. . . ."

"Sorry," Madison mumbled. She sniffled and took another sip.

"No, don't apologize!" Mom said. "I just have a lot on my mind, that's all. You asked. I'm the one who's sorry . . . for being so . . . busy."

"Oh," Madison said again. She pulled a blanket up over her.

"You know what? You look pale," Mom commented.

"But I always look pale, don't I?" Madison replied meekly.

Mom tucked the blanket snugly around Madison and moved the orange laptop off the bed. "I want you to close your eyes, honey bear. No e-mails right now. You need your shut-eye. Get some sleep before supper. Your dad is coming over tonight, remember?"

"Oh, yeah," Madison said. He was planning to bring over take-out food. Dad always either took Madison to dinner or brought burgers over before heading out of town.

"I can call him and cancel," Mom said. "If you want. . . ."

"No, that's okay. If Dad comes you can get more work done," Madison suggested. "You can just leave us and make your calls or whatever."

"That might work out," Mom said. She sounded relieved for the first time in their conversation. "Are you sure it's okay?"

Madison nodded enthusiastically. Ever since the Big D, when her parents got their divorce, Madison always felt strange about Dad's visits. When the visits started, it was awkward just having him come to the front door. These days, Mom didn't seem to mind if Dad came to the house for longer stretches of time. Madison always laughed at Dad because he knew (more than Mom) where everything in the house was located—from crayons to Scotch tape to pots and pans and the French roast coffee beans he loved.

Phin let out a low growl. He wanted to get up on the bed next to Madison.

"Can dogs catch bronchitis?" Madison asked aloud as she reached down to the floor and lifted up the pug.

"I doubt it," Mom said. "Besides, Phinnie is Super Dog, right?"

Madison smiled. Mom kissed her forehead.

"Oh, honey bear, it feels like you still have a fever," Mom said, sounding concerned. "You're sure you'll be okay if I go make a few phone calls?"

Madison nodded. "Uh-huh."

Mom kissed her again and replaced the empty box of tissues next to the bed with a full one. "If you need something, just holler. I love you."

"I'll try to sleep, Mom," Madison said. "Don't worry so much."

As soon as her mom left the room, however, Madison forgot all about sleep. Instead, she grabbed her laptop and powered it up again. While Phinnie curled up into a little ball and snored, Madison surfed onto bigfishbowl.com in search of a chat room and her two BFFs.

The three found one another in a room called ACHOO.

<Wetwinz>: my ears ache BAD

<MadFinn>: poor Fiona :~(~~

<Balletgrl>: I'm soooo wiped

<MadFinn>: poor Aimee :~(~~

<Wetwinz>: hey didn't u go 2 the doctor Maddie?

<MadFinn>: he said I have bronchitis does that sound serious?

<Wetwinz>: Dr. West sez I have a cold that's all

<Balletgrl>: I only have a cold 2 but the doc told me 2 sleep and stay home as much as possible BLAHHHH

<Wetwinz>: my mom sez she's worried

<MadFinn>: ur mom always worries

<Wetwinz>: I can't even leave the house if I have a fever

<MadFinn>: quarantine?!!

<Balletgrl>: that's harsh

<Wetwinz>: I wish Chet were the one who was sick he is being SUCH a pain having friends over grrrr to work on that 7th grade project tonite

<MadFinn>: friends? Like who?

<Wetwinz>: just DAN and HART

<Balletgrl>: OMG Fiona u have to find out if hart likes Maddie u HAVE TO!!!!

<MadFinn>: no way : ")

<Wetwinz>: that is such a good idea

<Balletgrl>: u can eavesdrop or read the computer

<MadFinn>: Aim Y R U saying this stuff? For the record I don't care what Hart thinks

<Balletgrl>: ur such a bad liar maddie u totally care

<MadFinn>: I DO NOT

<Wetwinz>: too bad I can't really ask Hart n e thing since Mom has me stuck up here in my bedroom like a gerbil

<Balletgrl>: U can still keep ur ears open though

<MadFinn>: is anyone else's head woozy RN???

<Wetwinz>: *wink*

<MadFinn>: pleez CTS!!

<Balletgrl>: ok ok ok chill out maddie

<Wetwinz>: what r u doing tonite?

<MadFinn>: Dad's coming 4 dinner too bad im not hungry

<Wetwinz>: r either of u going 2 school tomorrow?

<Balletgrl>: nope what about u?

<MadFinn>: I dunno yet prob not

<Wetwinz>: so let's meet online

```
tomorrow morning on bigfishbowl
<Balletgrl>: ACHOO2
<MadFinn>: sounds good
<Wetwinz>: *sniffle*
```

Madison clicked offline just in time to hear Mom coming back upstairs. With one movement, Madison lifted the blanket at the end of her bed and tossed it over the computer. She curled up into a knot and pretended to doze.

"Maddie?" Mom whispered as she pushed open the door.

Madison moaned in her fake sleep.

"Honey bear, your father is downstairs," Mom said. "He came by with some food. He's waiting in the kitchen."

Madison opened one eye and then the other. "What?" she said, even though she'd heard every word. "Did you say something, Mom?"

After Mom told her a second time, Madison slipped out from under her blanket and pulled on a Far Hills sweatshirt.

"Let's go, Phinnie," she said, hoisting the pug into her arms and heading downstairs.

Dad waited in the kitchen with several bags full of goodies. The whole kitchen smelled as though it had been deep-fried. He had brought chicken and biscuits from the Chicken Coop, a new fast-food chain that had opened near his apartment building.

"Hey, Dad," Madison sniffed the air and sneezed.

"Oh, Maddie!" Dad stretched his arms open wide. "You really are sick!"

"Did you think I was faking?" Madison asked.

Mom chuckled to herself and poured a glass of wine. "Want a glass of white, Jeff?" she asked him in a sweet voice.

Madison had noticed that with their divorce now more than a year in the past, Mom and Dad were able to get along better. Were they on their way to becoming *friends*?

"White wine? Fran, you know I'm not drinking," Dad said curtly. "Ever."

Mom rolled her eyes. "I can't remember everything," she said.

Dad sighed. "That's for sure," he said.

"Don't start this, Jeff . . ." Mom started to say something but cut herself off.

Dad was boiling under the surface, Madison could tell. Dad's not drinking was something important that Mom had obviously pretended to forget. And in a matter of seconds, Madison's parents had gone from cordial to cranky.

"Hey, Dad, did you get any corn on the cob?" Madison asked as she peeked into one of the greasy bags.

Dad slapped his own forehead. "No! I forgot!"

Mom rolled her eyes again and laughed softly. "Well, I'll leave you two to your chicken," she said, disappearing out of the kitchen toward her office. "Love you, honey bear."

She walked out with her glass of wine and a bowl of chips and clicked the lock on the office door behind her.

"Sorry, Dad," Madison said. "I mean, sorry that you have to come here when I'm sick. I know it's hard seeing Mom in the house and everything. . . ."

"Nonsense! I love being back," Dad said, looking fondly around the kitchen. "I remember when we had these countertops installed." He ran his hand over the surface. "Great space for cooking here."

Dad was a real gourmet, Madison thought. At least he was a gourmet compared to Mom, whose cooking skills were best described as a cross between "boils water" and "burns toast." Dad was always trying new recipes. If there was anything good about the divorce, it was the weekly dinners with Dad.

Madison picked at a piece of chicken. She wasn't hungry.

"Do you have a fever?" Dad asked, feeling her hot forehead. "Feed a fever, starve a cold, right?"

"Actually, I think it's the other way around, Dad," Madison replied.

"I always mess that up," he groaned, half laughing. Taking a huge bite of fried chicken, he changed the subject. "So, is Mom being a good nurse?"

"Well, Mom is really busy with work," Madison

24

said in a low voice so that her mom wouldn't hear. "You know how that goes. . . ."

Dad bit his lip. "I wish I could take care of you, Maddie. It's just that I can't miss this business meeting tomorrow. Wait! If you're sick, maybe you could stay with Stephanie."

Stephanie was Madison's brand-new stepmother. And although Madison liked her very much, she didn't like the idea of asking Stephanie to nurse her back to health. Stephanie wasn't *really* Madison's mother, after all. Wasn't that a job for her *real* mom?

"Just forget it," Madison said, trying to sound convincing. "I'm okay at home. I understand that you both have jobs. You're busy. . . ." Inside, a little voice screamed, *Tell him the truth! You want attention! You want TLC! You want warm cocoa! You want chicken soup! You want it NOW!*

"Maddie," Dad went on. "Are you sure?"

"Dad," Madison said. "I'm really fine. I swear, I'm not even that sick. . . ."

Gack! Hack! BLECCH!

Madison coughed. It wasn't an ordinary sputter. It was a long, dry, tickling cough that wouldn't stop no matter how much water or medicine she swallowed.

Dad slapped her on the back.

"Maddie!" Mom came rushing into the kitchen. "Are you okay? What's going on in here?"

Dad rubbed Madison's arm. She finally stopped coughing.

"I think maybe I should go up to bed," Madison said. "This bronchitis doesn't feel so cute anymore."

"Very funny," Dad said.

"Maddie, I want you in bed," Mom said, as if she were giving an order. She handed Madison two pills. "And take these."

First, Madison helped Dad clear the dirty dishes and wrap the leftovers. Of course, Dad still remembered the drawer where the plastic wrap and containers were kept. Madison gave him a huge bear hug before leaving the kitchen.

"E-mail me from your hotel?" Madison asked.

"I'll E you *and* call you. The doctor should have all of his test results by then, too, right?" Dad asked, kissing the top of her head as he had when she'd been younger. "I want you to get well quick, sweetie."

"I will, Dad," Madison said, pausing for a moment. She secretly hoped he would change his mind and stay.

But he didn't.

"Okay! I'm going to bed, Mom," Madison announced, leaning over the banister. "Are you happy now?"

Mom and Dad both chuckled at that one.

"Maddie, be nice to your mother, will you?" Dad said in a sterner tone.

26

Mom smiled. "Thanks, Jeff," she said.

"Lub you," Madison said through her stuffy nose. She blew them each a kiss and promptly sneezed again. It seemed like old times for a brief moment, as she stood there on the bottom step: Madison, Mom, Dad, and Phinnie, together again.

But it wasn't old times. The Big D had changed everything forever.

"Rowooororoorooooo!" Phin howled from upstairs. He'd raced ahead.

As soon she climbed to the top, Madison disappeared into her room. But despite her promise to Mom, she still didn't have sleep on her mind. Madison booted up the laptop again and headed into her e-mailbox.

She hit NEW MAIL.

```
From: MadFinn
To: Bigwheels
Subject: FEVER!
Date: Mon 22 Sept 8:56 PM
```
My fever is almost 102. But I can't sleep. I can't eat. And lucky me, my dad came over tonite and he and Mom got into some weird non-fight. That's how they do it. They're mad but they don't really yell. They just talk all around stuff. I hate it!!!!

How r u? How is Sparkles? How's
that guy Reggie u like so much? I
guess I have a lot of questions
today. Must be the cold medicine.

Madison stared off into space again. The medicine was definitely working better this time around. Her nose wasn't so runny anymore. She gazed right past her desk and out through her bedroom window. Streetlights illuminated the sidewalk in front of the house next door. Someone was out walking a dog.

Madison didn't recognize the dog or the dog walker. She got up and went to the window for a closer look. It was a boy. He had red hair, or at least it appeared red under the street lamp. He wore an old corduroy jacket, ripped jeans, and lumberjack boots. The big dog sniffed madly at a hydrant.

"Phinnie," Madison asked as she lifted the pug up to the window. "Do you know that dog?"

Phinnie wriggled loose and leaped to the floor. Apparently, he didn't know the mutt. And he wasn't in the mood to look out of windows. Phin just wanted to curl up on a pillow somewhere.

As Madison squinted to get a better look at the boy, he and his dog walked right into the neighboring house.

Madison gripped the windowsill and took a deep breath.

Who was this guy? Why had she never seen him before?

Madison touched her cheeks. Her face felt flushed. Was this another cold-medicine hallucination?—or had she really just discovered that a cuter-than-cute boy lived right next door?

For a brief moment, Madison didn't feel all that sick.

Chapter 3

"The doctor's office called," Mom said as she brought a tall glass of cold orange juice into Madison's bedroom on Tuesday morning. She raised the blinds and pulled back the curtains. "And it's a good thing you're staying home from school. Dr. Pinkerton says you officially have bronchitis. You will be out for a few days."

"What?" Madison asked, rubbing her eyes. Mom's words drifted over her like a thick fog.

Phin, who had followed Mom into the bedroom, jumped up and licked Madison's nose. Madison swatted him away.

"How are you feeling this morning?" Mom asked.

"Okay, I guess," Madison said. But as soon as she started to sit up in bed, she let out a long moan. Her shoulders drooped. "Oh, that was a big lie, Mom. I feel awful."

Mom reached out to feel Madison's forehead. "Yup," she said. "You're burning up."

"I feel ten times worse than yesterday," Madison rasped. "How is that possible?"

Mom shook her head. "Have some OJ," she said. "And take your medicine."

Madison took the juice and the medicine. She gave the top of Phin's head a pat. He rolled over to have his tummy rubbed, too.

"Maddie," Mom said. "I need to talk to you about work. . . ."

"Yeah?"

"Well the thing is . . . I have a few important appointments this week that can't be skipped," Mom explained. "And with your being sick, and your father being away, I'm in a tricky spot. . . ."

"Why?" Madison asked. "I can watch myself during the day. No prob."

"During the day is fine. But I have to go away for a night or two," Mom admitted finally. "And someone needs to take care of you when I can't be here."

"Do—you—really—have—to—go—away?" Madison asked, coughing between every word. She fell backward among her pillows and pulled the quilt up to her chin. She was still feeling hot and cold at the same time, just like yesterday.

Mom plumped up the covers around Madison.

"Well, I have a surprise for you," she said. "I called Gramma Helen. She's flying in from Chicago to help us out."

Madison's jaw dropped. She couldn't believe Mom had convinced Gramma to come all the way to Far Hills just to nurse Madison back to health. It was true that Gramma Helen had been saying for almost a year that she would visit, but then she had thrown her hip out and decided against traveling east. She was always making excuses about why she wouldn't get on a plane.

"Gramma?" Madison said, blowing her nose loudly. "I guess I can deal with that. When is she coming?"

"Tomorrow," Mom said.

"Tomorr—" Madison sneezed before she could get out the words. The sneeze sounded like an elephant's call.

"Let me go make you a cup of tea with honey," Mom said. "And how about breakfast? What do you want to eat?"

Madison made a yucky face. "No food. No tea," she said, sticking out her tongue. "I just want to lie here."

"Okay, Maddie," Mom said gently. "I'll get your tea later. But drink some water, will you? You need to stay hydrated. I'll be downstairs if you need me."

As soon as Mom left, Madison kicked off the blankets and dragged herself over to the window. She peered out. The bright air outside looked warm

32

and inviting; it was like one of those perfect September days that still feel like summer.

And she was stuck with a cold.

Madison looked across the yard to the neighbor's house where she had spotted the cute mystery boy the night before. She tried to guess which window was his. She wondered about his name. Where did he go to school? With each question her head spun. The medicine was kicking in.

Madison crawled back under the covers and closed her eyes tight. The only sounds in her room were the low rumble of Phin's shallow doggy breaths and her own squeaky breathing.

Within seconds, she was fast asleep.

Madison blinked because the sun was pouring in through her window and her face felt hot. She imagined herself getting sunburned while lying sick in bed. That would be funny!

The clock next to Madison's bed said 4:06. She'd been asleep longer than an entire school day.

"Phinnie?" Madison asked aloud, looking under the blankets for her pug. But he was no longer in the bedroom.

Madison took a sip of water from the cup on her nightstand. Then she reached down to the floor and pulled her orange laptop into bed with her.

Once the laptop purred on, Madison connected to the Internet and opened her e-mailbox.

FROM	SUBJECT
✉ Xcr_ultywQ	DON'T MISS THIS
✉ DantheMan	Lizard Alert
✉ TheEggMan	Hmeowrk
✉ newsflash88	Get Rich NOW
✉ Bigwheels	Sorry UR Sick
✉ GoGramma	My Visit!!!

Madison immediately deleted the messages marked DON'T MISS THIS **and** GET RICH NOW. **Then she opened a note from her good friend Dan. In addition to being a classmate at school, Madison and Dan volunteered together at the Far Hills Animal Clinic.**

From: DantheMan
To: MadFinn
Subject: Lizard Alert
Date: Tues 23 Sept 3:33 PM
Someone told me ur sick. No way
b/c I am @ the clinic & there
are 5 lizards here right now and
they are sick 2!!! I had 2 tell u
b/c u always laff @ stuff like
that.

Some guy collects exotic animals or
something & they all got the FLU so
his whole collection is HERE. Dr.
Wing put them in the cages way in
the back. I named them already:

34

Wizzy, Fizzy, Dizzy, Tizzy, and
Lizzy (of course).

Write back if u get bored.
See ya, Dan

Madison made a mental note to write back to
Dan about the funny lizard names. Then she clicked
on the message after his.

From: TheEggMan
To: MadFinn
Subject: Hmeowrk
Date: Tues 23 Sept 3:41 PM
hey maddie I volntered in scool
2day 2 get homework assns 4 fiona
and then I said I would 4 u 2 I
hope that's ok I will clal l8r bye

Egg

ps I will prob get 4 aimee if she
wnts

pps u need 2 decide who ur doing
that web project with topics r due
soon

Egg was the worst e-mail speller on the planet,
Madison decided. She chuckled to herself. And of
course he was getting Fiona's homework! He was

acting so mushy around Fiona lately. His reminder about the Web project set Madison's mind spinning. She had to e-mail Aimee and Fiona so that they could decide on their topic.

Madison took another sip of water. She didn't feel like her normal self for so many reasons. Her nose was clogged. Her head pounded. Plus, she actually felt popular today—she felt more popular staying at home sick than she did when she went to school in good health!

"I have to get sick more often," Madison sniffled to herself.

The next message was from her keypal. Madison had written to tell her about the mystery boy next door. Bigwheels had a lot to say on that subject.

```
From: Bigwheels
To: MadFinn
Subject: Re: FEVER!
Date: Tues 23 Sept 3:58 PM
That is so weird what u wrote me
about a guy next door. I have a
neighbor who is a boy, too, but he
is the opposite of cute. How can
someone live so close but u never
even notice him? Maybe your boy
just moved in. Send more info! BTW
what's up w/Hart these daze? U
don't mention him as much as b4. R
U still crushing on him?
```

Life here is ok. But I'm having
trouble in math already which is a
drag cuz math can be a good subject
4 me. Oh well. My 2 cats r GREAT.
How's Phinnie? The other day I was
in the mall and Pets Central had a
baby pug in the window. I thought
of u. :>)

I hope you feel better VERY VERY
VERY soon. It is so yucky to be
sick. At least u & ur friends can
all be sick 2gether tho. You
should have a sick sleepover LOL
with cocoa and videos. Write back
soon.

Yours till the puppy dogs,

Vicki aka Bigwheels

Gramma Helen had sent the final e-mail. She had
written to say that she loved Madison very much and
was glad to be coming to Far Hills to help out.
Madison smiled at the thought of seeing her grandmother. It had been a while. She hit DELETE. She
didn't need to save this one. After all, Gramma
Helen would be in Far Hills tomorrow.
Bleeeeeeep.
Her laptop made a noise. Insta-Message!

Madison hit REPLY and started to chat with her friend Lindsay.

```
<LuvNstuff>: w8! aren't u supposed 2
   be sleeping?
<MadFinn>: I am sleeping RN LOL
<LuvNstuff>: ha ha RN I'm up in the
   library media ctr.
<MadFinn>: y ur at school soooo late
<LuvNstuff>: *yawn* I have a lotta
   work
<MadFinn>: got n e gossip?
<LuvNstuff>: ur asking ME? Get real.
<MadFinn>: well . . . how's Hart?
<LuvNstuff>: QT AU
<MadFinn>: what else? Have u seen PI?
<LuvNstuff>: Poison Ivy? Yeah she
   was here 2day w/her drones which
   is weird b/c like 1/2 the school
   is sick
<MadFinn>: its so cool ur telling me
   about school while I'm home
   in bed I wish I could stay more
   connected
<LuvNstuff>: I should e you during
   the day
<MadFinn>: really?
<LuvNstuff>: totally
<MadFinn>: did u email Aim & Fiona
   yet
<LuvNstuff>: nope i wrote u first
```

```
<MadFinn>: thx
<LuvNstuff>: I miss u 3 soooo much
<MadFinn>: IKIK me 2
<LuvNstuff>: bye
<MadFinn>: bye
```

As Madison signed off, she blew her nose. It was fun reading all the e-mails, but her head was clogged. She needed more sleep. Mom was right. Madison quickly exited her e-mailbox and placed the laptop back on the floor.

"Mommmmm!"

Madison screeched as loudly as she could, so Mom could hear her, all the way downstairs in her office.

"Mommmmm!"

Madison called out once more, and then she snuggled under the covers, rubbing her bottom lip with the satin edge of a purple blanket.

Mom appeared a few moments later.

"What is all the fuss?" Mom asked, poking her head into the room. Phin trotted inside, too.

"My ears are ringing," Madison said.

"I'm sorry you don't feel well, honey bear," Mom said.

"And my throat is killing me," Madison said.

"Oh, sweetheart," Mom said. Then Mom spied the laptop on the floor. "Um . . . what's this? Have you been resting—or writing to your friends online?" she asked.

Madison looked down. "No," she answered.

"No, *what*?" Mom asked.

"No, I haven't exactly been resting," Madison admitted.

Mom clucked her tongue. "Maddie . . ." she said, sitting on the edge of the bed. "I told you . . ."

"I feel dizzy," Madison said aloud. A picture of Dizzy the lizard at the animal clinic popped into Madison's head. She giggled to herself.

"Well, lie down," Mom said. "I'm going to get you some food, whether you like it or not. I don't want you to start passing out. You need your sleep, Maddie."

Madison curled up into a ball and called for Phin to jump up onto the bed next to her. Her whole body ached. As Mom fussed with blankets and put away folded laundry, Madison wondered what the boy next door was doing right at that moment. Was he outside, right then, walking his dog?

Unfortunately, Madison was way too exhausted to get up and peer out the window. She'd be on the lookout as soon as she caught a few *z*'s.

Madison crawled back into bed. As she buried her face in a cool pillow, she wondered if maybe *all* high temperatures were not so bad.

After all, what was really making hers rise?

Was it the bronchitis that gave Madison her fever?—or was it a certain someone who lived next door?

Chapter 4

The next morning, Mom raced around the kitchen, frantically wiping down counters and sweeping the corners of the floor. Her behavior meant only one thing: Gramma Helen was arriving soon. Madison knew the real truth: Mom didn't want Gramma to come into the house and start noticing dust bunnies. Gramma was a stickler for a clean house. Mom wanted everything to look perfect.

"Slow down, Mom," Madison said as she slurped her OJ. "You're making me dizzy."

"I thought you were *already* dizzy," Mom joked.

The phone rang. Gramma had just picked up her luggage. She was hopping into a cab at the airport. Mom wanted to pick her up, but Gramma had insisted on taking a taxi to Blueberry Street.

Although Madison felt woozier than woozy for the second day in a row, she was starting to get excited about Gramma's arrival. Mom had been so busy with work projects that she hadn't had much time to spend with Madison. That made being sick a little lonely. But now Gramma would be there to play cards with Madison and give her all the TLC she needed.

At least, that was the plan.

Madison hung out by the front door waiting for Gramma's taxi to pull up. "Gramma!" Madison yelled, pulling her bathrobe around her tightly. "You're here!"

"My Maddie!" Gramma shouted back as she made her way onto the front porch. "Oh, my little angel! Look at your nose, it's all red!"

Madison *knew* she looked like Rudolph, but Gramma was the only one who admitted it. Madison leaned in and gave Gramma a hug.

"What's this? You're not wearing any slippers? Get yourself back inside, before you catch your death!" Gramma said.

Madison wrinkled her nose. "Gramma, it's almost seventy degrees out here. I'm practically sweating."

"Well, that's because you're sick. Now, shoo!" Gramma said.

Madison had to laugh. Gramma always got worked up over the silliest stuff, like slippers.

"You know, last week I was having take-out

42

Chinese with my good friend Mabel and I got the strangest fortune cookie," Gramma said, walking into the front hall and removing her jacket.

The taxi man followed behind her with a large, red suitcase. Gramma tipped him before he disappeared.

"What was I saying?" Gramma sputtered, taking off her yellow chiffon scarf and placing it gently in the sleeve of her jacket.

"Fortune cookies?" Mom laughed. She appeared in the hallway, arms crossed. "Hello, Mother."

"Oh, Frannie dear!" Gramma said. "I was telling Madison about a fortune cookie I got just last week. It said that I would travel to a faraway place to help a loved one. Isn't that something? And here I am."

"That's pretty cool, Gramma," Madison said. She liked the fact that Gramma Helen believed in fate and karma and things like fortune cookies.

Madison did, too.

"Thanks for coming, Mother," Mom said, reaching for Gramma. They squeezed each other. Mom took Gramma's bags into the living room.

Madison felt a tickle in the back of her throat. She started to cough . . . and cough. . . .

"Goodness!" Gramma said, rushing over to feel Madison's forehead. "You sound horrible! Frannie, how can you let her out of bed in this condition?"

Mom smiled. "I'm not sure how to answer that, Mom."

Madison laughed, which only made her cough more.

Mom got her a glass of water.

"Listen to that racket! It's a good thing I'm here," Gramma said.

"Uh-huh, Mother," Mom said. "Now why don't we get Madison back in bed? Then you and I can catch up a little."

"Can't I stay downstairs with you both?" Madison asked. She plopped down on the sofa.

Gramma shook her head no. Mom shrugged.

"We could grab some blankets and get you set up on the living room sofa," Mom suggested.

"Rooooooooooooooof!" Phin barked. He liked *that* idea.

"Nonsense! You should get some sleep in your own bed," Gramma said, raising her eyebrows and giving Madison one of her "listentomerightnow" looks.

Madison smiled. "Okay, Gramma," she said. Madison wanted Gramma Helen to feel that what she said mattered, since she'd traveled all the way from Chicago on a moment's notice.

"See, Fran?" Gramma said smugly. "She listens to me."

Mom didn't react. She gave Madison a sidelong look. "So let's go back upstairs to bed, then," Mom said.

Madison nodded. "Fine." She got up and started toward the stairs.

Even though Madison wanted to stay with Gramma and Mom, being back in her bedroom wouldn't be so awful, after all, she thought. She could go online and check her messages, visit bigfishbowl.com, and surf the Net. And maybe she would sleep—just a little. Madison was feeling a little weak in the knees from her medication and all that coughing.

Phinnie tagged along, as usual. He dragged his favorite rope toy upstairs. Madison promptly removed it from her room. It was wet and chewed-on and smelled as though it had been sitting at the bottom of a moldy garbage can for weeks. Madison couldn't stomach that smell on an ordinary day. It was even worse when she felt sick.

She'd been in her bedroom for only a few minutes when Gramma appeared at the doorway. Madison hadn't fallen asleep yet, much to Gramma's dismay.

"My stars!" Gramma said, barging into Madison's bedroom. "You're still up? Get into bed this instant!" She chased Madison toward the bed.

"Gramma," Madison said firmly. She wanted to insist that Gramma just leave her alone, but realized that wouldn't have been very smart. Gramma had come all that way—just for her. And the truth was that Madison had wished for lots of attention.

Maybe I should have been more careful about what I wished for? she mused.

Gramma sat on the edge of the bed and started to rub Madison's back.

Madison started coughing again.

"That sounds so awful," Gramma said, rubbing harder. "What you need is a saltwater gargle."

"A what?" Madison said, gulping. "*That* sounds awful."

"Not at all," Gramma said. "It's good for you."

That was what grandmothers said about everything gross they wanted you to do when you were sick, Madison thought. *It's good for you.*

"I brought my compact cold-air vaporizer from Chicago," Gramma went on. "It's good for your sinuses and breathing."

Madison nodded.

"And tonight I think you should take a long, warm bath. I have this eucalyptus bubble bath that smells great," Gramma said.

"Why don't we play cards?" Madison asked.

Gramma shook her head. "Not now," she said. "You are going to get some sleep." Gramma went over to the window and drew the curtains. The room got darker.

"It's like night in here," Madison said.

"That's the idea," Gramma replied.

Madison nestled under the quilt as Gramma gave her a gentle kiss on the forehead.

"It's a good thing I'm here," Gramma said for a second time.

Madison nodded. "I know," she said, and rolled over. Gramma walked out of the bedroom, shutting the door behind her.

As soon as she was gone, Madison sat up. Since she couldn't do much of anything (including breathe) without having a coughing fit, the best activity wasn't even sleep. So Madison decided to surf. She booted up her laptop again.

Madison felt like a spy in the darkness of her room. The screen flashed and filled the room with a dim, blue glow.

She had e-mail in her mailbox.

Hooray!

During her morning free period, Lindsay had written to Madison, Aimee, and Fiona from the media lab at school. Reading it was like being back at FHJH.

From: LuvNStuff
To: MadFinn; Wetwinz; Balletgrl
Subject: Mega Gossip
Date: Wed 24 Sept 10:37 AM

I am sitting in the library right now with a perfect view of you-know-who. Yes, I'm talking about Miss Wishes-She-Were-All-That, otherwise known as POISON IVY. First of all, she is wearing this truly UGLY brown shirt with fringe

on it (no I am not kidding) and
jeans that are WAAAAAY too tight.
I know she's skinny and I'm not a
fashion plate myself but these
are UGLY pants. So I was in the
stacks earlier and I overheard her
and the drones talking. Can we
just say for the record please that
Rose and Joanie are the two most
ANNOYING people on the planet?
They do not have minds of their
own, they just agree with everything
Ivy says. But anyway Ivy was up
here talking about Hart because
(drumroll please) he BLEW HER OFF
yesterday.

I heard that Ivy & Hart were
supposed to get together during
lunch yesterday (after you 3 went
home sick) to study or talk about
that Web page project. Well, he
never showed! And even worse (or
better!), he told this other kid
Ross that he doesn't even WANT to
do the project with Ivy. OMG!
Somehow Ross told Phony Joanie her
dronie--and now Ivy knows and WOW
she is SO MAD. Maddie, this is HUGE
news, right? I mean, maybe this
means Hart really is yours and all

yours!!! Whaddya think? Maddie + Hart
4-Ever!

In other school news, some kid set
off the school alarm this morning and
Principal Bernard had a MAJOR fit.
Asst. Principal Goode was
running around the halls looking
for the guilty party. I think it's
some ninth grader. Well, that's the
theory in school anyhow. There are
always a lotta rumors about this
stuff. It hasn't been boring around
here even though I MISS YOU GUYS!

I hope you are all feeling better. I
wish I could be in bed watching TV
all day. BTW: Egg told me that he's
getting homework for Aim & Maddie. He
said he can drop it on your porch in
the mailbox or somewhere. And I guess
Chet is obviously getting yours, F.
If you need ANYTHING please just E
me. I know you already picked each
other to do that Web project but I
was hoping I could join with you
three. Would that be okay? 2 is
company, 3 is a crowd, but 4 is
AMAZING! I made that up. LOL.

I will send another update VVS (like

same time tomorrow). If you need
any special info, just lemme
know.

BYE-BYE!

Lindsay

Madison's mind (and heart) raced. Hart had
blown Ivy off? That was news. Thrilling, exciting,
amazing, WOW news.

But Madison didn't know if she should feel
glad—or sad. After all, Hart might have blown Ivy
off because he liked someone else. . . . But what if it
weren't Madison? What if it were Carmen or some
other cute girl in their class? There was no way to
know for sure.

Madison placed her laptop on the bed for a
moment so she could get up and get a tissue. The
box beside her bed was empty.

Prrrrrffffffffff! Prrrrrffffffffff!

Madison blew her nose hard and walked over to
the window.

The house next door stared back at her, empty.
There was no boy outside walking his dog. Madison
wondered if maybe he went to school somewhere
other than Far Hills. Maybe he was older? Maybe he
was visiting from out of town?

She needed to find out who he was.

Prrrrrfffffffffff! She blew her nose again.

"Maddie?" Gramma Helen's voice cut through Madison's thoughts.

She whirled around to face her grandmother.

"Not so hard!" Gramma warned. "You'll blow a blood vessel in your eyes if you blow that hard, not to mention your nose."

"Sorry," Madison replied sheepishly, wiping her face. She coughed for effect, which made her cough for real.

"Listen to that!" Gramma said. "I just came up to see how you were feeling and to find out what you wanted for dinner."

"Dinner?" Madison answered. "Gramma, it's only lunchtime."

Madison noticed that Gramma was wearing orange rubber gloves that stretched up to her elbows. She smelled vaguely of bleach.

"I'm trying to get things in order around here," she said.

Madison could almost see Mom rolling her eyes as Gramma rewashed everything Mom had spent hours scrubbing that very morning.

"Gramma," Madison said. "What are you cleaning for? Why don't we just play cards or something? Why don't you just chill out?"

"No time for chilling out. There are things to be done," Gramma said.

"What things?" Madison asked.

"Your mother needs my help," Gramma replied. Madison nodded.

"Besides, don't you want me to make you some chicken soup?" Gramma asked. "And clean up the house so we can have some fresh air around here? This place is a little stuffy, don't you think?"

Madison nodded again. "What kind of chicken soup?" she asked, trying to change the subject.

"Chicken and lemon and orzo," Gramma said as she shooed Madison back into bed. "Now, you stay bundled up, and I'll be back in a jiffy."

Madison smiled. "Okay," she said simply. There was nothing else she could say.

Luckily, Gramma had not noticed the laptop at the side of the bed. Madison's flatfoot platypus screen saver wasn't blinking very brightly in the dark room. Madison lifted it back onto the bed. She had a little while to stay online before Gramma returned with the soup.

Another e-mail was waiting.

```
From: Bigwheels
To: MadFinn
Subject: For You!!!
Date: Wed 24 Sept 10:46 AM
I found the coolest Web site with
free cards u can download. So I am
sending one to you. It's attached
to this e-mail. Yours till the nose
blows,
```

Vicki aka Bigwheels

<attachment>: GET WELL, GIRL (card)

The greeting card was animated. Bigwheels had two cats of her own, so she sometimes sent cards and notes with cat's-paw borders. This card had two kittens playing with a ball of multicolored string that spelled out the words "Get Well, Girl!" as the string unraveled.

Madison hit REPLY.

From: MadFinn
To: Bigwheels
Subject: Re: For You!!!
Date: Wed 24 Sept 12:51 PM

Ur amazing! THANKS SOOOOOO MUCH. I love it when u send me cards and poems like that :>)

I am still feeling ickier than icky but now my Gramma is here so I feel a little better. Mom has to go away for business for two nights and that stinks because I like having Mom around when I'm sick, don't you? But Gramma will fill in for her and I can deal.

BTW you asked about Hart & he's the same. I haven't seen that cute guy

again next door but I am looking
out for him too. I had this dream
last night that he was spying on me
and wanted to meet me. I wonder if
we ever will meet? I wonder if I
will ever even know his REAL name?

Write back or else! I am semi-bored
already and I've only been home
sick for two and a half days.

Yours till the cough drops,

Maddie

Chapter 5

<LuvNstuff>: thks for letting me do the project w/u

<Balletgrl>: :-)

<Wetwinz>: sorry we didn't ask right away

<MadFinn>: is everyone ok with optical illusions as our topic???

<Balletgrl>: Yup we can do some groovy stuff on the Web page like show actual illusions with wavy lines and circles

<Wetwinz>: I already plugged the topic in a search engine and got a lot of hits

<MadFinn>: I found this magic book

on my mom's shelf and it gave me
some other ideas
<LuvNstuff>: we should have info for
all subjects like science, math,
and not just one
<Balletgrl>: grrrrreat idea
<Wetwinz>: I'm sorry u can't come
over now. chet is doing his
project with hart and dan I think
they're writing about ships or
something
<LuvNstuff>: kool beans

The four friends chatted for almost half an hour about the project.

Lindsay and Fiona would collect information on magic and optical illusions. It was a broad subject, so they were trying to figure out how to narrow it down. Lindsay suggested they call the page *Playing Tricks on Your Eyes* so it could include sleight-of-hand tricks as well as plain old optical illusions.

Aimee would collect images. She would ask her dad (who owned the Cyber Café in downtown Far Hills) to help out. Mr. Gillespie knew what art the girls could use with and without permission. Some pictures couldn't be downloaded because they belonged to other people or organizations. Madison didn't really understand copyrights, but she knew she and her friends would have to be careful with whatever they posted on the Web.

As the computer pro of the foursome, Madison was in charge of pulling everything together and formatting the page. As much as she had wanted the challenge, it seemed like an overly daunting task, especially when Madison could barely think straight. Where would she begin? Where did anyone begin?

After signing out of the chat room, Madison opened a new file.

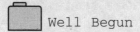 Well Begun

Gramma Helen once showed me this little card in her purse that said, "Well begun is half done." Some classical philosopher named Horace said that. It's a good thing that things in my life have been well begun. I think. Unfortunately, most of these are a long way from being half done-- or even started, for that matter.

1. I need to do all this reading for English class. I have only been out of school for two and a half days and I'm already chapters behind in *The Outsiders*. And oh yeah, don't forget math, science, and Spanish class homework. HELP!

2. I've been picked by my BFFs as the one to put together our optical illusions Web page. They're doing a lot of the work, but somehow it feels like I'm the one sure to be left holding the bag.

Or holding the mouse, I guess. I'm a
little scared that I can't do it.
3. Gramma has all these unrealistic rules
   about what sick people (like me) can and
   cannot do. Rule #1: No leaving the house
   with a bad cough. (Um . . . that means
   I'll be housebound for weeks!!!) Rule
   #2: In bed for at least a day after a
   fever breaks. Rule #3: No wet heads
   after a shower. And on and on. Of
   course THIS is not the way I wanted to
   spend our visit. I don't want more
   rules!

Rude Awakening: Face the facts: how can
anything be WELL begun when I feel soooo
SICK?

Madison was about to hit SAVE when she heard
footsteps. Her fingers froze on the keyboard.

"Maddie, dear?"

Gramma!

Madison hit a few keys to escape her file. But the
laptop was working slowly today. And she didn't
have time to move it off the bed before Gramma
came striding in.

"What's that you're doing?" Gramma asked. Her
eyes scrunched together as she stared down at the
laptop.

Madison felt warm all over—and it didn't have
anything to do with her bronchitis or fever. It was a
reaction to Gramma's steely look.

"I . . . um . . . well . . . I was just . . ."

"Tsk, tsk. Maddie!" Gramma clucked. "You are supposed to be having a nice rest, not playing games."

"It's not . . . I mean . . . I can't . . ." Madison stammered.

"There's a boy downstairs to see you."

"A boy?" Madison's face lit up. "To see *me*?"

"He said his name is Egg," Gramma said. "What kind of a name is that?"

"It's my friend Walter, Gramma," Madison said, her face drooping. She had no idea why Egg would have been dropping by.

"Did I meet this boy the last time I visited? Why are boys calling on you when you're sick in bed?" Gramma asked.

Then it dawned on Madison. Egg was coming over with homework.

Madison got out of bed and slid on her monkey slippers. She didn't want Gramma to give her a hard time about having bare feet. She pulled a sweatshirt on over the T-shirt and sweatpants she'd been lounging around in.

"Where are you going?" Gramma asked.

"Downstairs to see Egg," Madison replied.

"Like that? But you're sick."

"Gramma, it's only Egg," Madison said, covering her mouth as she coughed between words. "I won't talk for more than five minutes, I swear."

Gramma threw up her hands. "Okay," she said

with a smile. "And *then* you can take your nap. Right?"

"Right."

Madison smiled back and quickly sped downstairs to see her friend.

"Keep back," was the first thing Egg said when Madison came to the door.

"Thanks a lot," Madison said.

"Hey, I don't want your slimy germs," Egg added. "Here are your homework assignments. I was going to leave 'em on the porch, but then your Gramma opened the door when she saw me out here and . . ."

"You're *such* a good friend. . . ." Madison said sarcastically.

"Fiona was right." Egg said. "She said you were the sickest out of the three of you. And you look pretty sick. But then again, you always look sick. Ha!"

"You really know how to cheer me up, don't you?" Madison said.

Egg snickered. "I'm just kidding. Lighten up."

Madison leaned against the doorframe and crossed her arms. The air outside was warm. She inhaled deeply.

"Okay. I have to go," Egg said, taking a step backward.

Madison reached out as if she were going to grab him and give his arm a twist, but something caught her eye. She stopped.

The boy next door was there on the sidewalk. He was raking leaves.

Madison ducked back into her doorway. Egg looked over at the boy.

"What's wrong with you?" he asked. "Who's that?"

"Some guy," Madison said. "I don't know."

"Wait," Egg said. "I do. He goes to Far Hills Junior High. I've seen him around the halls. His name is Joe or John or something. He plays hockey, I think. Drew knows him a little."

Madison's stomach lurched. The boy next door went to her school? She had never seen him before.

"You know him?" Madison asked.

"Wait, it's Josh, I think," Egg said, thinking out loud. "Yeah, Josh. That's his name! He's in ninth grade."

Madison grinned. "Ninth grade? Really?" she asked.

"Why don't you just ask him yourself?" Egg said, gesturing toward Josh. "He's *your* neighbor."

Madison folded her arms in front of her and stepped to one side. She had to be one hundred percent sure Josh could not see her stained sweatpants and bird's-nest hairdo.

"What . . . do you *like* this Josh guy?" Egg teased.

Madison could feel herself blush deeply. "Like him? No, of course not. I was just asking a question. That doesn't mean anything," Madison said.

"What about Hart?" Egg asked.

61

"Hart?" Madison said, almost losing her balance. "What are you talking about?"

"I thought you dug Hart," Egg said.

"Who told you that?" Madison asked, knowing instantly that of course it had been Fiona, who confided everything in her "boyfriend," Egg.

Egg rolled his eyes. "Come on, Maddie," he said dramatically.

"What else do you know?" Madison asked.

"Everything," Egg cracked.

Madison bristled. "Well . . . does Hart know?" she asked.

"Know what?"

"Egg! Does Hart know . . . that I like him?"

"I think so. But so what? He doesn't care," Egg said.

"He doesn't care?" Madison asked. Even though a part of her was moving on to a new crush, her heart sank when she heard *that*.

"I don't know what he thinks. We don't really talk about it," Egg said.

Madison tried to read Egg's expression to see if he was making stuff up or not. She couldn't tell.

"Maddie!" Gramma called out behind her. Madison jumped.

"I better get going," Egg said, starting down the porch steps the moment Gramma appeared.

"Thanks *a lot*," Madison said.

Egg waved quickly at Gramma and dashed off.

"You should be sleeping. . . ." Gramma said, rubbing Madison's shoulders.

Madison's head bobbed. The shoulder rub felt good, especially because the bronchitis made her feel a little achy. "Okay, Gramma, I'll go back to bed," Madison said.

Instead of getting under the covers when she got upstairs, however, Madison opened the curtains at her window. She looked outside to see if Josh were still there raking.

He was.

The afternoon sunlight shone on Josh's head as he moved around the yard. Now that she looked at him in the daylight, Madison saw that his hair was actually more brownish than red, but still, she liked the fact that his hair had orange highlights. Orange was her favorite color on the planet, after all.

"I wonder if he knows that I live next door?" Madison wondered aloud. She looked down at Phin. He was nuzzling her ankle. "Do you think a ninth grader would ever notice *me*, Phinnie? Do you think . . . ?"

Blip-blip. Blip-blip.

Madison shot a look at her laptop. It was still on? She'd forgotten to turn it off when Egg arrived. Now it was beeping to tell Madison that she had an e-mail message.

Blip-blip. Blip-blip.

Madison sat on the edge of her bed. She hit a

random key on the keyboard and the screen came into view. A small icon flashed in the corner of the screen: NEW MAIL.

Madison opened her e-mailbox and selected the new message. She smiled when she saw the screen name.

From: Bigwheels
To: MadFinn
Subject: Don't Be Bored
Date: Wed 24 Sept 3:11 PM
How r u feeling?

I know what u mean about being
bored when ur sick. There's nothing
worse. N e way, during a VERY
boring American History class I made
up a list of 10 things 2 keep u from
losing ur mind when ur sick. Ready?

(Sorry if it's dumb)

Madison giggled. She heard an imaginary drum-roll in her head.

1. Turn on the tube and zone.
2. Eat chocolate. Lots of it.
3. Make something with glitter.
4. Turn up the radio.
5. Laugh at ur Dad's bad jokes.

```
 6. Read a book about a faraway
    place.
 7. Put on ur snuggly old sweat
    shirt.
 8. Think about Hart. :>)
 9. Think about that other cute guy.
    :>)
10. Send e-mail to ur keypal ASAP.
11. Bonus one for Maddie: HUG
    PHINNIE!!!!

Yours till the temperature drops,

Vicki aka Bigwheels
```

"Excuse me?"

Gramma stood at the bedroom door with her hands on her hips.

"Madison Finn," Gramma shouted. "You said you were coming up here to take your nap! And now I find you on the computer again? Goodness!"

Madison swallowed hard. "Yes, Gramma," she said. "I left it on . . . and . . . then I got this new e-mail and . . ."

"Show me how that thing works," Gramma said.

Madison was stunned. That wasn't the response she'd expected.

"Show you what?" Madison replied. "But, Gramma, you know how it works. It's like your computer at home."

"Oh, no," Gramma insisted. "My computer is a dinosaur that sits on my desk. Yours looks way too fancy for me. It's orange, for goodness' sake! Can you send e-mails from that thing?"

"Sure," Madison said. "That's what I've been doing the last two days, while I've been sick. That's why I wasn't exactly sleeping when you thought I was. Sorry."

"I see," Gramma said thoughtfully. "So could I send e-mails to my friends?"

Madison grinned. "Sure. Do you want to?"

Gramma grinned back. "Oh, my neighbor Mabel just got a computer and I promised her I'd write a note or two while I was away. She checks her e-mail every morning. Always forwarding me these joke e-mails and chain letters. It's a good way to pass the time."

"Gramma, you're way more high-tech than I thought," Madison said.

"Well, you helped me out with that," Gramma said with a wink.

"So, let me show you how to send e-mail from my address," Madison said, moving over on the bed to give Gramma room.

Gramma moved a little closer.

"I'm so glad to be here with you," Gramma said softly, leaning in to kiss Madison on the forehead.

"Me, too," Madison said. "Thanks for coming to Far Hills."

She leaned back on her pillows and pressed a few keys. Before long, Madison was showing Gramma bigfishbowl.com, the FHJH Web site, and every other online place that mattered to her.

Sitting on the quilt with Gramma's arm around her shoulders, Madison felt as though she must have been getting better, even though she still felt slightly feverish.

Chapter 6

Phin had crawled under the table. Even he sensed that something was wrong.

Madison stared straight down at the waffles on her breakfast plate. Thursday mornings at home were not usually this complicated.

"Mother, I'm not sure that you're listening," Mom said, leaning against the counter with a cup of hot coffee in one hand and a piece of dry toast in the other. "Or else I'm not explaining myself well enough to you."

"No, you've explained perfectly. And I understand that you have work to do, but . . . but . . ." Gramma couldn't finish her sentence.

"But what?" Mom said, taking a bite of toast.

"But . . . I wonder if you have your priorities in order," Gramma finally said. She clapped her hands together. "That's all."

"That's *all*?" Mom answered. "Mother, that is most definitely NOT all. However, I don't think we should discuss this in front of Madison."

"It's okay, Mom, I'm not really listening," Madison said.

Mom threw back her head. "No, honey bear, this doesn't concern you. . . ."

Gramma's face soured. "It absolutely does concern her, Francine!" Gramma never called Mom by her full first name unless she was upset.

"You're right," Mom conceded. "But I don't want to discuss it now. Okay?" Mom placed her empty coffee cup into the kitchen sink and washed her hands. "I'll see you later, honey bear," she said.

Gramma sat down with her bowl of pink grapefruit sprinkled with brown sugar and her cup of hot tea. She didn't say anything more, not even when Mom disappeared into the next room.

"Gramma?" Madison asked after a brief silence.

"Maddie?" Gramma replied, taking a bite of fruit.

"Did you want to do something together today?" Madison asked. "Like play cards? Or maybe send more e-mails to your pals back in Chicago?"

"You still have a terrible cough. I think you should stay in bed," Gramma said, wagging her finger in Madison's face. "Besides, I don't want to catch whatever it is you have, do I?"

"So? We can hang out in my room," Madison said. "Mom's going out for her meeting. We can hang out and I can stay in bed at the same time. And later this afternoon we can go to Dr. Pinkerton's office."

"I don't know, Maddie," Gramma said. "You should rest."

"I'm not contagious anymore! "Madison insisted. "And I promise I won't sneeze on you."

Gramma sighed. "Okay. We'll play cards. Let me clean up and do a load of wash first. I'll be up in a few minutes." She handed Madison a tablespoon of cough medicine.

Madison promptly swallowed the liquid and grabbed Phin. They headed upstairs to Mom's bedroom. Madison threw herself across the unmade bed. She stretched out and watched Mom dress for her meeting.

"Mom, are you going to be back for dinner?" Madison asked.

"I know it's bad timing, honey bear," Mom said, shaking her head no. "But this documentary needs some serious work. We have a lot to do. . . ."

"I understand," Madison replied, sniffling.

"How's your headache?" Mom asked. "I hope I don't catch your bug."

"It's more like a full-body ache," Madison said.

"And it's still here. I feel more awake now, but I have the chills a little."

Madison buried her face in one of the down pillows. She waited for Mom to come over and feel her forehead again. She always did that compulsively when Madison was ill. Madison wished Mom would drop everything and hug her tightly. Hugs always took a little of the ache away. But Mom was busy putting on her earrings and wrapping a scarf around her neck.

"Isn't that Gramma's yellow scarf?" Madison asked when she glanced up from the pillow.

Mom nodded. "She lent it to me. Do you like it?"

"You look like Gramma," Madison answered.

Mom smiled. "I do?"

"Yeah, Mom," Madison said. "You look pretty."

Madison waited for Mom to look over and blow a kiss, as she always had when Madison was younger. But there was no kiss. Mom raced into the bathroom instead.

"So, I won't be back for dinner—and then I have this trip over the weekend—" Mom shouted. "But after that I'll be back home, and we can spend some more time together. I promise!"

"Uh-huh," Madison said.

Mom came out of the bathroom. Madison expected her to bypass the bed again, but this time Mom stopped in front of it and flung her body next to Madison's so hard that the bed bounced like a trampoline.

"Move over, honey bear," Mom said.

"Mom!" Madison cried. "What are you doing? You'll mess up your hair and outfit. You'll catch all my cooties, remember?"

"I don't care," Mom said.

Madison felt a warm sensation inside the center of her chest, as if Mom were finally giving her a hug from the inside out.

"I love you, Mom," Madison said, sniffling.

"I love you, too," Mom replied, giving Madison a kiss. She stroked Madison's head.

Phin jumped onto the bed and started licking Madison's neck. She squirmed away, giggling.

"Do you want to stay here under my covers?" Mom asked.

"Nah, I'll go into my room," Madison said. "But thanks."

Just as Madison was about to leave Mom's room, the portable phone rang.

"Aren't you going to pick that up? I'm sure it's for you," Mom said. "I'm not expecting any calls."

Madison grabbed the phone. It *was* for her. Fiona was on the line.

Fiona had called to let Madison know that she couldn't work on the Web site project that day, because the family computer at the Waterses' house had crashed. She also informed Madison that Aimee couldn't do much work, either. Her fever spiked, *and* she was throwing up—a lot. Madison winced.

She hoped she wouldn't contract those symptoms.

"Maybe Lindsay can do some work on the page?" Fiona suggested.

Of course, Madison knew that Lindsay might have a conflict of interest. She had *another* important project she was working on: Operation Junior High Spy. Since Madison couldn't get information firsthand, She had asked if Lindsay wouldn't mind reporting back on gossip at school. The only trick was that Lindsay had to gather all of the information secretly. No one could know why she was asking questions—especially questions about a mysterious ninth grader named Josh.

And so the BFFs' optical illusions page would have to wait.

After getting off the telephone with Fiona, Madison sent Aimee an e-card with little basset hound puppies on it; that was the same breed of dog as Aimee's dog, Blossom. Blossom had recently had puppies of her own. As Madison was sending it, a message from Lindsay popped up on-screen. It was marked TOP SECRET, with a little red exclamation point.

```
From: LuvNStuff
To: MadFinn
Subject: TOP SECRET
Date: Thurs 25 Sept 11:02 AM
Okay. The mystery guy's name is
Josh Turner (BTW: it's not Joshua
```

either, just Josh, if that matters
to you at all). He is in ninth
grade. He plays hockey and he plays
the accordion AND tuba (isn't that
bizarre? Who plays the accordion
except polka bands?) But this guy
Josh isn't in marching band or
anything. I only know about the
music because I overheard him
talking to someone in the caf.
Maybe he was actually just making a
joke. Hmmmm. I followed him twice
in school today when I saw him by
the lockers and he was wearing a
ripped cord jacket with patches on
it. I think he looks a little like
a TV actor, but I don't know which
one. He was alone both times I saw
him (i.e. no girlfriend!) What else
do you want to know?

xoxoxoxoxoxoxoxo

Lindsay

p.s.: I know Aim is feeling really
lousy so we haven't started on the
project but that's ok b/c I heard
in school today that they're
planning to make a big extension to
the whole class on this project.

Yeah! Fiona sent me e-mail and said
she's feeling ok. How about u???

Madison coughed when she read the last part, as if testing herself to see how she *was* feeling. Unfortunately, the one dry cough turned into a whole coughing fit.

Gramma appeared at the bedroom door, looking worried. "We should head out to Dr. Pinkerton's office," she suggested.

"But my appointment isn't until later," Madison said.

"Let's get you out of the house—and over to your doctor, now," Gramma said. "The fresh air will do you some good."

They said their good-byes to Mom again and left Phin in the kitchen with a half-filled bowl of kibble, a full water dish, and an actual dried pig's ear, a disgusting snack that Mom had picked up for Phin at the supermarket.

Dr. Pinkerton's office was packed. Although outside it was a beautiful day, it seemed as though all of Far Hills had contracted the flu.

Madison and Gramma sat in the waiting room for more than an hour before a nurse took them in to an examining room, where they waited for another half hour. The room smelled like antiseptic. Madison flipped through an issue of *Good Housekeeping* magazine. She found a funny article about celebrities and their dogs. Two different stars in the article had pugs—just as she did—but their pugs weren't nearly as cute as Phinnie.

When they finally got in to see Dr. Pinkerton, he said that Madison's bronchitis was still bad but that it would slowly disappear over the next few weeks. He told her that cough medicine alone wouldn't do much good, which surprised Gramma.

"The best medicine is hot tea and sleep," he said.

That made Gramma smirk. It was such a Gramma Helen thing to say. The doctor reported that, happily, Madison didn't have any other major flu or bronchitis complications. Even though she'd been feeling hot, Madison's fever was gone, and she would not be throwing up anymore. She didn't need to return for any more visits unless there were an emergency.

Once they were back in the car again, heading home, Madison started coughing again.

"I go to the doctor, and he says I'm getting better. But then I'm out of the doctor's office for five minutes and I'm sick again! How is that possible?" Madison moaned.

Gramma shrugged. "Murphy's Law," she said.

"Who's Murphy?" Madison asked.

Gramma chuckled. "It's just an expression. It means that if something can go wrong, it will."

"No matter what Dr. Pinkerton says, when I start

coughing I feel like I'm going to be sick *forever*," Madison said.

"Nonsense," Gramma said as she drove toward home. "Just give yourself a chance to get better. You've only been out of school for two days. You need your sleep, just as the doctor said. . . ."

As they drove along, Madison gazed at the round sun sinking behind clouds. Madison loved September nights—the way the sky turned deep orange and pink. She could see the speckled landscape of bright stars even though the sky had not yet fully darkened.

"We were at the doctor's for a long time," Madison said. "I wish they hadn't made us wait so long."

"What should we have for supper?" Gramma asked. "How about chicken soup with ribbon pasta, or maybe chicken vegetable?"

"Chicken? Again?"

Madison chuckled to herself. One predictable thing about being sick was the menu: soup, soup, and (surprise!) more soup.

Mom was still not home when Gramma and Madison arrived. They ate soup and toast with Phin, played a few games of Crazy Eights, and settled in for the night. Madison put on cotton pajamas with rose and fuchsia-colored confetti circles; they were like a designer pair Madison had seen in a teen magazine. Gramma wrapped herself in a big, hand-knit cardigan. Together, they watched a romantic, made-for-TV-movie and each laughed whenever the other cried at the sappy parts.

By the time Mom arrived at home, Gramma had nodded off in the reclining chair.

Madison heard Mom go into the kitchen. She followed her.

"Hi, Mom," Madison said. "You're late."

"I know," Mom said, leaning toward Madison for a kiss. "What have you two been doing all day? Where's Gramma?"

"Asleep," Madison replied. "We hung out today. Went to see Dr. Pinkerton. My bronchitis is still pretty bad, so I guess I have to stay home from school another day," she coughed. She told Mom exactly what the doctor had said.

Mom nodded. "That's why Gramma is here. Extra TLC."

They heard Gramma stir in her chair in the next room. She was snoring. Madison and Mom could hear her all the way in the kitchen.

Madison giggled.

"Why don't you head up to your bedroom, Maddie?" Mom requested. "I'll wake up your grandmother in a few minutes."

Phin led the way upstairs. Madison was going to check her e-mail, but decided against it. Gramma was right. She did need some sleep.

Madison wandered over to close the curtains. As

she stared out the window toward the house next door, she thought about her mysterious neighbor. Why hadn't Madison ever seen Josh Turner at FHJH?

There weren't any lights on next door, so Madison assumed that Josh and his family were out for the night—until a bright yellow lamp clicked on downstairs.

Madison bit her lip as she watched a light go on in an upstairs window, too. She saw someone move in the shadows. She could see a bed, a night table, and . . . a person . . . stepping into the light . . . with slightly reddish hair. . . .

Yes!

It was Josh.

Madison grinned when she realized that he was there, wandering around in the half darkness of his bedroom. She sat down on the window seat and started to think about what it would have been like to meet him face to face. Had he ever noticed Madison at school? Had he ever looked through *her* window?

No!

Madison froze. Josh had his nose pressed up against the glass of his window. He was staring toward her room.

Quickly, Madison ducked behind her curtains.

When she leaned around to peek over at his window again, he waved.

Tentatively, Madison waved back. She fought

hard to hold in her nervous giggles. What was happening here?

Josh held up a finger as if to say, "Hold on one moment!" and dashed away and out of sight. A moment later he returned to the window with a piece of yellow cardboard in his hands. On the cardboard was a message in black Magic Marker.

HI THERE

Madison almost fell over because she started laughing so hard.

HI THERE? It seemed so normal—but still weird.

Josh shrugged and waved the sign again, looking for some kind of response.

Madison was about to search for a pen and paper on which to write her own sign back, but she stopped. There were footsteps on the stairs. She couldn't risk getting caught by Mom or Gramma in the middle of her window "conversation"! What should she do?

Phin nipped at her knees. Without a moment's hesitation, Madison closed the curtain and jumped back. A few moments later, when Madison realized that she'd been hearing things and that no one had entered Madison's room, she gently pulled back the curtain again, hoping to see another yellow sign.

But by then the light in Josh's bedroom had been turned off. He wasn't there. Madison collapsed on her window seat.

"Where did he go, Phinnie?" Madison asked aloud.

Phin let out a little bark, as if he wanted to climb into the window seat with Madison. She picked him up, pulled him into her lap, and gave him a cuddle.

Josh Turner. Josh Turner. Josh Turner.

Madison said his name over and over in her mind. Finally, they had made contact. *He* had made contact. With a sign!

For a person as superstitious as Madison, it was all about the signs.

She wondered what the next one would be.

Chapter 7

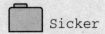 Sicker

Last night I went to sleep dreaming of dreamy Josh Turner. I was thinking about what will happen when I head back to school next week. Maybe I'll see him in the hallway and he'll ask me to have lunch with him at his table in the cafeteria. That would just burn Poison Ivy if I got to sit with the ninth graders at lunch!

While I was thinking about all this, I got SICKER! I had a massive coughing fit and spent half an hour trying to stop this awful tickle in my throat. Gramma had to make me hot peppermint tea with honey. That

was really nice of her but it was A MAJOR
DRAG because after coughing for soooo long,
I started to get this thumping headache. And
to think, I thought I was getting better!!!
I have the cold sweats, too. Gross. And
Gramma said (of course) all of this is
because I tried to do too much before I was
better. There's nothing worse than someone
who says, "I told you so." Ugh. So why do
moms and grandmoms always say that?

Rude Awakening: Just when I thought I
was off and running--major relapse. Now I'm
just *cough* and running.

The funny thing is that I called up
Fiona and Aim and they both had a relapse,
too. Fiona said she's not moving out of bed
and her Dad moved the TV into her bedroom.
And Aimee's mom made her these all-natural
health elixirs from stuff like alfalfa and
wheatgrass and chamomile. Gross.

Maybe I better listen to Gramma Helen
next time she tells me how to get better.

Madison looked over at her bedroom clock. She
debated whether or not to call Fiona or Aimee
again, but decided against it since she'd already
spoken to her BFFs twice that day.

Madison was starting to feel claustrophobic. She
still had not changed out of the confetti-print pajamas
from the night before, and her hair felt a little greasy.
Being sick usually meant being lazy, especially when
it came to clothes. Madison could live in the same

T-shirt for a day. . . . or two . . . or more. But even she had to admit it was becoming grosser than gross. She'd take a shower later, she decided.

Madison was putting off the shower for the moment so that she could log on to her laptop again. Since she'd gotten sick, Madison had been spending a lot of her time online.

```
FROM              SUBJECT
☒ JeffFinn        How's My Girl?
☒ Bigwheels       Hope Ur Feeling Better
```

Madison was happy to see that Dad had sent a get-well-soon e-mail. She missed him.

```
From: JeffFinn
To: MadFinn
Subject: How's My Girl?
Date: Fri 26 Sept 9:09 AM
```
How do you cure a headache? Put your head through a window and the pane will disappear--HA-HA-HA! Like I told you on the phone, I've been swamped at meetings the last 24 hrs or so. I'm off to see another client in a few minutes! But I miss you so much. I've been thinking of you. Stephanie says you haven't called so I assume that means you and Mom and Gramma Helen have things under control. Good!

What did the doc say after your
second checkup? I'm coming back
after the weekend so we have to
plan dinner and a sleepover at our
place when you feel good. That way
I can make up for not being there
to give you TLC right now.

I love you so much. Give Phin a hug
for me.

Dad

Bigwheels had sent an e-mail, too. Madison couldn't believe it when she opened it up. The note was short and sweet with an attached musical message. When Madison clicked on the message icon, the song "Raindrops Keep Falling on My Head" started to play while Bigwheels's words scrolled across the screen:

I said to get better soon. So what
happened?

Yours till the coffee cakes, Vicki
aka Bigwheels.

Madison chuckled. She was about to hit REPLY when an Insta-Message popped up.
It was Lindsay. She was writing from the media

lab at school. Madison guessed it was Lindsay's free
period.

<LuvNstuff>: ur online!
<MadFinn>: *^_^*
<LuvNstuff>: I HAVE BIGBIGBIG NEWZ 4
    U!!!
<MadFinn>: Tell me!
<LuvNstuff>: this is a super scoop
    r u ready? Hart was asking about
    YOU today at school
<MadFinn>: Get out
<LuvNstuff>: seriously I heard him
    by the lockers
<MadFinn>: Get out x2 what did he
    say??
<LuvNstuff>: he asked Dan if you
    were feeling better or not and he
    looked really concerned I swear
<MadFinn>: y would he ask Dan?
<LuvNstuff>: I dunno good question
<MadFinn>: well that's not really a
    big deal, is it? I mean we ARE
    friends
<LuvNstuff>: yeah but there's more.
    I was in the lunchroom & I saw
    something else MAJOR.
<MadFinn>: what happened?
<LuvNstuff>: ok lemme start at the
    start. Hart was sitting w/Egg and
    Drew for a while and then he got

up and went back to get dessert
or something. On the way he
passed Ivy Daly's table and as
usual she threw herself at him.
She wanted him to stop and talk.
And not only didn't he stop or
talk BUT I heard him say to Egg
when he got back to the table
that Ivy was a pain. He actually
used the words "annoying" and
"attitude" and "go away" in the
same sentence. I almost fell on
the floor. I swear, I almost
cracked up. I really & truly
thought he liked Ivy. Didn't u
say that he liked her?

<MadFinn>: he DOES like her
    otherwise why would he always
    hang with her during free periods
    or lunch? I don't believe u

<LuvNstuff>: I knew you would say
    tht but IT'S TRUE!!!

<MadFinn>: I can't get my hopes up
    about HJ

<LuvNstuff>: Y not? If he doesn't
    like Ivy I bet he likes YOU

Madison took a deep breath. She paused at the
keyboard, unsure about what to write next.

<LuvNstuff>: maddie r u still there?

87

```
Have 2 go 2 my last class
<MadFinn>: oh sorry I was thinking
<LuvNstuff>: I'll E u l8r tonite,
    ok??
<MadFinn>: tx for the gossip
<LuvNstuff>: I love being ur spy
    :-)
<MadFinn>: TTYL
```

Madison's head whirled. She was beginning to wish her Hart crush were still a secret. Plus, she had a new guy on her mind now.

Josh.

She didn't really know Josh, but a little voice inside Madison's head told her that he was someone special. She imagined what they would look like together, walking down the street with their dogs. Having a ninth grader boyfriend would be cooler than cool.

Maybe even cooler than Hart, Madison thought.

Madison closed her eyes and tried to picture Josh hugging her. She pictured his brown eyes (that was a guess—she didn't know his real eye color—yet), his broken-in sneakers, and his leather jacket. What kind of real date would they go on? Where would Josh take her? What would she wear?

Since she didn't feel like writing back to anyone or looking up information for their optical illusions project, Madison perched on her window seat with her legs crossed, her eyes on Josh's window. He would be home from school soon, Madison hoped. She waited and waited, hoping for a glimpse.

Maybe he had a tuba lesson? Madison snickered. She couldn't picture that cute ninth grader stuck behind an enormous musical instrument like a tuba.

Madison glanced outside. She spotted someone headed toward the front porch.

Egg! Madison picked herself up and went downstairs to see what he wanted, but before she could intercept him, he had come and gone. She found Friday's packet of homework on the porch with a simple note that said, *Here you go. See ya. Egg.*

Madison picked up the homework and dumped it on the hall chair. She couldn't do math problems now. She needed to get back upstairs to spy on Josh. He'd be home soon.

She was about to head upstairs when she heard voices. Mom and Gramma were in the kitchen talking. Their voices seemed to get louder. Madison stood just outside the kitchen door, eavesdropping.

S*he* was acting like a super spy now.

"Mother," Madison heard Mom yell at Gramma. "I don't know what that has to do with anything. I told you my work on this documentary is important."

"As important as your kids?" Gramma asked.

"Kid," Mom corrected her. "I have one."

"And now you *have* to go out of town?" Gramma asked.

The room was silent. Madison wondered why Mom hadn't answered. She peered around a corner.

"I hate leaving," Mom said. "But yes, I really *have* to go."

"I don't understand you sometimes, Francine," Gramma said.

"Well I don't understand why you have to put me on the defensive, Mother! Can we just drop it?"

Madison's stomach did a flip-flop. She hated arguments. It reminded her of the times just before Mom and Dad had divorced, when they had argued at least twice a day.

Madison popped into the kitchen. "Hi!" she said cheerily, trying to catch them off guard. It used to work well with Mom and Dad. It seemed to work okay with Mom and Gramma, too.

Mom grabbed the counter. "Oh! Maddie! How long were you standing there, honey bear?"

"Standing where?" Madison asked, playing dumb.

"We were just making dinner," Gramma said, humming a little.

"Oh, yeah . . ." Mom said. "Dinner." She moved around the counter and reached into a cabinet for a big pot in which to boil corn on the cob.

"Were you just outside?" Gramma asked. "I thought I heard the screen door slam."

"My friend Egg dropped off my homework,"

Madison said. "I saw him from the upstairs window. I saw you, too, walking Phin."

"Oh, yes," Gramma said. "This pug and I have become fast friends again."

Phin let out a little whimper. He was curled up by his favorite place in the kitchen, which was next to the dishwasher during the drying cycle.

"I have to make a quick phone call, Mother," Mom said. "I'll be right back to help with the salad."

Gramma nodded as Mom left the room.

"So . . . how are you feeling?" Gramma asked Madison.

"You don't have to pretend," Madison said. "I heard everything."

"What are you talking about?" Gramma said, looking confused.

"I heard you and Mom arguing," Madison admitted. "Mom wasn't being very nice to you."

"Maddie," Gramma said gently. "Your mother is under a lot of stress right now."

"She never has time for me," Madison said.

Gramma's face looked stunned. "Is that what you really think?" Gramma asked. "Because she has to work a lot?"

Madison nodded. "Sometimes," she said.

"Hmmm," Gramma said. "Well, that isn't good. You can't walk around being secretly mad at your mother, can you?"

"Why not?" Madison grumbled. "I'm sick."

Gramma chuckled. "I guess you do. Maddie, try to understand that your mother is very busy right now. It doesn't mean she loves you less because she isn't here in the house all the time. Or because she sends for me when she has a work conflict. You *do* understand that, don't you?"

Madison gulped and nodded. She did understand. It just bugged her.

Gramma gave Madison a squeeze. "I'm here right now. What can I do for you?"

Madison squeezed back. "Nothing," she said.

Gramma started chopping up tomatoes. "Maddie, I think it's time to take your medicine." She handed her a little cup.

Madison took the pill and headed back upstairs to close her laptop and clean up her room a little bit. She hadn't coughed in almost half an hour. It was like a new world record. She was glad that Gramma had brought her portable vaporizer. That was making a big difference.

Josh's bedroom window was open. She didn't see any motion at first. But after a moment, out of nowhere, Josh appeared.

Madison grinned. Could he see her again?

The answer was obviously yes. Josh pulled up a yellow cardboard sign with one big, black word.

WHASSUP?

Madison giggled. She was more prepared to

communicate now than she had been the day before. Madison took a sheet of paper and wrote her own word back.

HELLO

Even across their two yards, Madison could see Josh's bright, wide smile.

He really was cute.

Josh held up another sign.

NAME?

Madison grinned. She briefly contemplated calling herself something different and mysterious, like Natasha, but in the end she wrote her real name.

MADISON

Then she wrote another question.

YOU?

Josh frantically scribbled his reply. Of course, Madison knew that answer in advance.

JOSH

They wrote one- and two-word notes to each other back and forth for a few minutes, mostly joking around. As they "chatted," the sun began to fade in the sky. Josh turned on his lamp. His room was flooded with yellow light. Madison walked away from the window for a moment to turn on her light, too.

When she came back, Josh was gone. His light had been shut off. His blinds were drawn.

This wasn't a good sign.

Madison stared and stared so long that she

thought her eyes might stay stuck wide open. Was he coming back again?

Phinnie barked. He chased his tail around in circles. He liked to do that sometimes when he was hungry. Madison played with Phin on the carpet, but kept glancing over at Josh's window—just in case.

No luck.

After dinner with Mom and Gramma, Madison checked the window again to see if Josh might have been there. When she didn't see any signs of life (or light), Madison crashed on top of the quilt on her bed and made a secret wish.

I wish that Josh Turner would fall madly in love with me.

Madison felt a little dizzy. Her eyes got heavier than heavy.

And soon Madison Francesca Finn herself was out like a light.

Chapter 8

When Maddie opened her eyes it was Saturday morning. Gramma stood over her, fluffing pillows.

"You fell asleep *on top* of the covers?" Gramma asked.

Madison was only half awake. "Yeah, yeah," she mumbled to Gramma. "I'm warm enough. Don't worry."

"Maddie, I'm here to worry!" Gramma insisted.

Gramma chased Phin out of the room so she could gather clothes from the hamper. She straightened the books on Madison's shelf.

Slowly, Madison dragged herself off the bed. "I don't feel so good, though," she said. "I'm achy again."

"Well, I'm not surprised," Gramma said. "You

probably caught a draft lying on top of the blankets instead of under them."

"Gramma, I already told you, I'm warm. Mom has the heat up."

"Tell you what! I'll make you one of my super-booster smoothies this morning. There's a load of vitamins in that shake."

"Okay," Madison agreed. "What day is it? Is it Saturday?" She'd lost track.

Gramma nodded.

"How's about I run you a nice, hot eucalyptus bath?" Gramma asked, fluffing Madison's pillows for a second time.

"Right now?" Madison shrugged. She'd never really taken a bath in the morning. "I don't know, Gramma," she said, walking over to her closet. She pulled her hair back into an elastic and slid into a pair of faded jeans and a comfy green T-shirt.

"Gee, if you're getting dressed, I guess that means no bath," Gramma said with a smile.

Madison smiled back. "Yeah. I guess."

"Well," Gramma fussed at Madison's top. "I just want you to get well, young lady," she said, poking at buttons and picking at a thread.

Madison squirmed. She hated the way Gramma was all over her this morning. And she dreaded the thought that her bronchitis was worse than before. That meant Gramma would keep picking and poking and running baths and vaporizers and . . .

"What else do you need, Maddie?" Gramma asked.

"Um . . ." Madison said. "I'm okay, Gramma, really."

"But you just said you're feeling worse," Gramma said, touching the top of Madison's head.

Madison wanted to run. Couldn't Gramma just leave her alone until she woke up?

"Let me go put a load of wash in the dryer," Gramma said. "Then I'll make you a yummy breakfast. Your mother leaves this afternoon."

"Whatever you say, Gramma," Madison said.

As soon as Gramma left the room, Madison scooted over to Mom's room.

"*Help!*" she said as she threw herself across Mom's bed.

"What now?" Mom said, stuffing a sweater into her suitcase.

"Mom, I love Gramma so much, but she is driving me crazy," Madison said. She blew her nose hard.

Mom chuckled knowingly. "Oh, Gramma comes on a bit strong sometimes," she said. "But only because she loves you."

"She wanted me to take a bath this morning."

"That's not crazy," Mom said. "You'd probably feel better."

"She doesn't like it when I'm always online or e-mailing my BFFs," Madison said.

"Really? She told me she thinks it's great that you have such a close group of friends," Mom said.

"Yeah, but she thinks it's weird that I have a lot of guy friends," Madison said.

"She does not. You're making that up," Mom said.

"Mom! Are you on my side or what?" Madison exclaimed.

"Who said anything about taking sides? This isn't a war, you know," Mom said. "Not even close."

Lying on her back, Madison crossed her arms and pouted. "Fine, then. Go. Have a nice trip."

"Maddie . . ." Mom's voice softened. "Is that what this is really about? Me going away when you're sick?"

Madison shook her head. "No."

"Then, what?" Mom asked.

"What am I supposed to say to Gramma when she's giving me all these weird homemade medicines she likes to make and putting hot cloths on my head and cleaning my room? Mom, she was *cleaning* my room."

"Maddie . . ."

"And I'm sick of soup," Madison moaned.

"Soup? Honey bear, Gramma is doing us a huge favor by being here. Don't let yourself get all worked up just because she's being overly nice. You should be grateful. I know I am."

"I love Gramma Helen," Madison said. "I don't know why she just bugs me sometimes."

"Well, if there's a moment when she bugs you,

just call me on my cell phone," Mom said with a wink. "I finally got it fixed."

"Do you really mean it?"

"Just think! While I'm gone, you and Gramma can talk about how much *I* bug you," Mom teased.

Kicking her legs into the air, Madison bounced up and off the bed. Mom had more packing left to do.

Madison hadn't been away from her own bedroom for very long. But in that short time, Gramma had refolded sweaters, straightened papers (including postcards tacked up on Madison's bulletin board), and made Madison's bed. She'd put Madison's teddy bears on display in a row by the pillows.

Madison hadn't had her bears on display like that since she was ten.

Mom poked her head into Madison's room. "Did you hear the doorbell?"

Madison shook her head. "No. Isn't Gramma downstairs?"

At that moment, Gramma appeared in the doorway, wearing a giant apron and yellow rubber gloves. "Isn't it good luck that I brought these with me?" she asked.

"I thought I heard a bell. Is someone at the door, Mother?" Mom asked.

"Oh, yes, a boy," Gramma announced. "For Madison."

"For me?" Madison said.

Madison's eyes bugged out. A boy? *Josh*

Turner? It had to be. Who else would be in her neighborhood on a Saturday—except for her neighbor?

"Are you expecting someone?" Gramma asked.

"Oh, I'm sure it's just Maddie's legion of secret admirers." Mom joked. She grinned and went back into her room to get ready.

"Mom! I can't believe you just said that!" Madison called out after her.

Madison looked down at her ratty jeans and top. Her hair looked like spaghetti. How could she go to answer the door looking—and feeling—like a total mess?

"Stall him, Gramma!" Madison said. "Please."

"I'll see what I can do," Gramma said, toddling back downstairs.

Madison tried to run a comb through her hair but it didn't help. She switched tops, too, but the second one looked as sloppy as the first. Madison's nose was red again, too, from sneezing all morning. And the tickle in her throat had returned. She felt another coughing fit coming on.

Maybe Josh wouldn't notice?

As she went downstairs and approached the front door, Madison thought to herself: this could be it. This could be IT.

"The guy of my dreams could be standing right outside and I'm about to meet him," she said softly to herself. "Hello, destiny."

Her heart thumped. She opened the door.

As she pulled the door toward her, the person on the outside pushed in.

Thunk.

The door flew open. It was a boy, all right, but not the one she'd hoped it would be. Egg stood there, not Josh.

She sighed. Egg was definitely not her destiny.

Egg had his hands wrapped around a fat textbook. The title on the book's spine read *Classic Short Stories and Poems.* He shoved it at her stomach.

"Here. I forgot to bring this yesterday with the other homework," Egg said. "It's from Mr. Gibbons's English class. We finished *The Outsiders.* Now we have to read some short stories in this."

Madison took the book.

"You didn't have to bring this over," Madison said, feeling grateful and dejected at the same time. "But, thanks."

"No prob," Egg said. "We were all over here in the neighborhood, anyhow."

"We?" Madison asked.

"Yeah, me, Drew, and Hart," Egg said. "We're going to Chet's."

"Huh?" Madison's jaw dropped. She had not seen the other boys standing there. They'd been waiting off to the side.

"How are you, Maddie?" Drew asked.

"Yeah, Finnster, how are you feeling?" Hart asked.

"Drew? Hart?" Madison's voice squeaked. "Wow. What a surprise."

Madison couldn't take her eyes off Hart. His hair was tousled and he had on a brown sweater that matched his eyes. She could only imagine what he thought of *her* outfit.

Just then, Phin ran outside. Goofing around, Egg and Drew chased him to the opposite side of the porch.

"Um . . . these are for you," Hart said. He held out a tall vase of flowers.

Madison stared.

"At least, I think these belong to you," Hart said with a grin.

Flowers?

"For me?" she asked, biting her lower lip.

Had her crush really shown up at her house . . . with a bouquet . . . with Drew and Egg standing right there to witness it all?

No way.

"Thanks, Hart," Madison said softly. "I mean . . ."

NO WAY.

"No one ever gets ME flowers," Egg teased.

"This was really nice of you. . . ." Madison stammered. "I mean . . ."

"Oh," Hart looked away. "No biggie. They were just sitting there on the porch step."

"Sitting there?" Madison repeated, taking the vase. "Where?"

"Look at the card," Drew suggested.

Madison felt for a teeny card attached to the bottom of the vase. She ripped open the envelope.

FOR MY SWEET GIRL, NO MORE GETTING SICK! LOVE, DAD.

Madison sighed. "The flowers are from my dad," she said.

"Duh. Who *else* would send you flowers?" Egg said.

Madison nodded. "Duh, of course," she said, looking right at Hart, even though he wasn't looking at her.

"Hey, Drew!" an unfamiliar voice rang out from the sidewalk in front of Madison's house. Everyone turned to see who was speaking.

Josh Turner?

Madison froze. She'd never seen him up close.

"Yo! Josh!" Drew said.

He strode onto Madison's porch.

"What's up?" Josh said, smiling at everyone, especially Madison. He turned to Drew. "You going to the hockey match today?"

"Nah," Drew said. "My team isn't playing. How about you?"

Josh nodded. "Oh, yeah, I have a game today and tomorrow. Big-league."

He looked way better up close than he did long-distance, through his window. It was enough to make Madison dizzy all over again.

"You play hockey?" Madison blurted out.

The boys all turned and stared at Madison.

"Maddie, what is your problem?" Egg asked. "You know we all play hockey."

"I meant . . . does Josh play?" Madison asked.

"Hello? He's only the biggest scorer in our district," Drew said, giving Josh another high five.

"Well," Josh said, humbly. "Sometimes I lead the practice for Drew's group. So, I was just heading out and saw you all standing here. . . ."

"Yeah, we were headed to our friend's house. We stopped to drop off a book for Madison," Drew explained.

"So, I'll see you around the rink, I guess," Josh said to the group.

"Maddie, you should come to a hockey game," Hart said.

"Huh?" Madison asked. "Game?"

Hart looked confused. "I said, you should come to a hockey game."

"Uh-huh," Madison answered Hart, but continued to stare at Josh. Madison thought about their secret sign conversations and smiled to herself.

"Well, I have to go," Josh said. "See you later, neighbor."

Madison blushed. "Later," she said.

As soon as Josh disappeared down the porch steps, Egg turned to Madison. "So, we have to get going," he said. Madison was grateful that Egg didn't mention anything about their having discussed Josh on Wednesday.

"That is so cool that you live next door to Josh Turner," Drew said. "He's such a good player."

"I bet," Madison said, dreamily.

"You never met him before just now?" Hart asked.

Madison shook her head. "Nope. Maybe I *should* go to a hockey game. . . ."

"You can come watch us play. We have practices this week," Hart suggested.

"When does Josh have his next game? Do you know?" Madison asked.

Hart frowned, but that didn't really register on Madison's radar. She was still recovering from the up-close-and-personal Josh encounter. Hart shoved his hands in his pockets.

"Let's go," Hart said to Egg and Drew.

Madison said good-bye to her friends and walked back into the house. Her head felt lighter. She couldn't stop smiling.

Then she passed a hall mirror.

"Oh, no!" Madison cried.

Gramma came running, still wearing her gloves and apron. "What's wrong?" she said.

"Look at my shirt, Gramma!" Madison shrieked.

In the center of Madison's T-shirt was a spot she hadn't noticed when she changed outfits.

And her hair looked greasier than greasy. Half of it was sticking out of her ponytail in the wrong direction.

Madison put her head in her hands and moaned.

"You don't understand, Gramma. That was HIM. The guy I like more than anything right now. And I look like *this*. I could die."

"Murphy's Law," Gramma said, rubbing Madison's back. "Just when you think something can't possibly go wrong—"

"It does," Madison said, finishing Gramma's sentence.

Chapter 9

"Pass me those onions," Gramma said as she stood by the oven making supper. "I'm making a feast, so watch out!"

"Here you go," Madison said as she rolled an onion across the kitchen counter. It ricocheted off the toaster in Gramma's direction.

Gramma laughed. "You make cooking much more interesting, Maddie," she said. "Good thing I didn't ask you to pass me a watermelon!"

Mom had left for her business trip hours before, so it was just the two of them hanging out—plus Phinnie, of course. Gramma always baked doggie biscuits for Phin on special occasions and sent them from Chicago. Now she was here to bake them in person! Phin drooled when he saw them come out of the oven, shaped like little dog bones.

Madison remembered what Mom had said about being grateful for Gramma's visit. As she sat in the kitchen watching Gramma make her special lasagna for dinner that night, she felt very grateful. But it wasn't just the food or the TLC. Gramma was a good listener.

"Did Mom ever date older guys?" Madison asked out of the blue.

Gramma nearly dropped the onion and knife. "Excuse me?" she said.

"Did Mom date older boys when she was my age?" Madison asked.

"Mom didn't *date*, period," Gramma replied. "Is this about those boys who came to the door earlier?"

"Well . . ."

"Don't you think seventh grade is a little young for boyfriends?" Gramma asked, slicing fresh tomatoes onto a tossed salad.

Madison shrugged. "Seventh grade isn't too young for Far Hills Junior High," she said. "Everyone dates."

"Everyone?" Gramma said, raising her eyebrows.

"Well, everyone except me," Madison said.

Gramma put down the utensils and walked over to Madison. She sat at the kitchen table and smoothed out the tablecloth.

"When your mother was younger, like around

108

your age, all she ever talked about was boys," Gramma said.

"She talked to you about them?" Madison asked with disbelief.

"I remember she had a terrible crush on one boy from her school. His name was Theo."

"Gramma, how can you remember his name?" Madison asked.

"Aha! I remember because your mother wrote his name everywhere—on her books, on her desk, on the back of her closet door, even! She got punished for that one," Gramma explained.

"Mom never talks about any of her old crushes," Madison said.

Gramma smiled. "She had plenty. You should ask her some time."

Madison giggled. "It seems weird to like a lot of different boys at once."

"Weird? NO!" Gramma said. "Don't believe any gibberish about crushes being meaningless or that it's bad to be boy crazy. That's nonsense. You be how you want to be. Like whomever you want to like. We all have our crushes!"

"Even *you,* Gramma?"

Gramma stood up again so she could take the lasagna noodles out of the pot. She winked at Madison. "I'll never tell," she whispered.

Madison burst out laughing. "Gramma!" she yelled. "You have to tell."

"Let's see . . . I used to dream about marrying this boy who lived right next door," Gramma admitted. "He was four and a half years older than me. Imagine that!"

"No way!" Madison said. She couldn't believe Gramma had had a crush on her neighbor. But four years older seemed way too old. Not like Josh. He wasn't too old, was he?

Gramma continued with her story.

"I was fourteen, and he had just graduated from high school. He was working downtown at a gas station, where we always saw him pumping gas and fixing tires," Gramma said. "On weekends he used to hang out on his front porch and wait for me and my friends to come outside. My goodness he was such a sweet talker!"

"What was his name, Gramma?"

"Oh . . . Charlie Francis," she said, batting her eyelashes a little. "I loved the way he wore his ties."

Madison couldn't imagine liking some guy because of the way he wore his tie!

"So what happened?" Madison asked.

"Two years passed. He kept flirting with me, but I didn't really take it seriously. But the very day I turned sixteen, he crashed my birthday party. He asked my father if he could take me out on a date."

"So, you were sixteen, and he was *twenty*?" Madison asked. "Whoa. What did your father do?"

"He threw Charlie out on his ear. But later on, my

father changed his mind. I guess Charlie fixed his car up real good. That clinched the deal. He decided that Charlie would make a fine date."

"That is such a great story," Madison said. "You're so lucky to have had someone like you that much."

"Oh, Maddie," Gramma cooed. "I think you worry too much about boys liking you. You are just right—and the right boy will come along."

Madison helped Gramma pour the tomato-and-ricotta mixture over the lasagna noodles.

"What else do you remember about Mom when she was in seventh grade?" Madison asked.

"She always talked about having kids. Loads of kids. I think her magic number was twelve."

"Twelve? But then why did she only have me?" Madison asked. "I never knew she wanted more kids."

"People change," Gramma said. "And they change their minds most of all."

"Mom changed," Madison said. "Didn't she?"

Gramma nodded. "Your mother is always changing. But she likes to work hard. I am very proud of her for that."

"If only she didn't have to work *so* much. . . ." Madison's voice trailed off.

"She loves you, Maddie," Gramma said, shoving the lasagna dish into the preheated oven.

"I know," Madison admitted. "I know."

111

Gramma pulled a deck of cards out of her apron. "Want to play while the lasagna bakes?"

Madison nodded, and they dealt hands for Crazy Eights.

"Speaking of boys . . ." Gramma said, while Madison was taking her turn. "I forgot to mention earlier that I saw one of your boyfriends in the yard when I walked Phin earlier."

"Boyfriends? Who?" Madison cried.

"The boy next door. Josh something."

"You saw him?" Madison asked.

Gramma nodded. "Gosh, I guess it was yesterday. He told me to say hello to you. I can't believe I forgot. With Mom heading out on her trip I got distracted."

Madison just sat there, slack-jawed. "What else did he say, Gramma?" she asked eagerly. "You have to tell me. What did he say?"

"Just hello," Gramma said. "Isn't that enough sometimes? He was thinking of you."

Gramma winked. Madison knew her secret about liking Josh was out in the open, right there on the kitchen table. But she also knew her secret was completely safe with her grandmother.

Four Crazy Eights card games later, Madison told Gramma more about liking Josh. Gramma divulged information about some of her long-ago crushes, like Mackie, the butcher's son, and a boy in her church choir named Gabriel. Madison sopped up the funny details like a sponge. She loved hearing about

Gramma's secret past and wondered how many times Mom had talked with Gramma about those kinds of things.

About a half hour before dinnertime, Gramma went off to take a nap. Madison retreated to her bedroom to boot up her laptop. She was pleasantly surprised to find her BFFs online again, and she Insta-Messaged Fiona and Aimee. The three met in a new chat room called ACHOO3.

```
<MadFinn>: is everyone feeling
    better???
<Balletgrl>: Not exactly did either
    of u puke?
<Wetwinz>: that is so gross Aim
<Balletgrl>: try DOING it I can't
    keep any food down
<MadFinn>: I bet it was that
    seaweed in your soup--ick
<Balletgrl>: But I love kelp!!!
<Wetwinz>: You need kelp help LOL
<MadFinn>: what does the doc say?
<Balletgrl>: I have 2 stay in bed
    today & tomorrow and maybe even
    miss school part of next week
<Wetwinz>: UR sooo lucky.
<MadFinn>: I'm looking 4ward to
    school
<Balletgrl>: sure b/c u wanna see
    HART
```

113

\<Wetwinz\>: Egg said u saw him today. What did he say???

\<MadFinn\>: nothing what was he supposed 2 say?

\<Balletgrl\>: I love u more than n e thing

\<Wetwinz\>: More than IVY

\<Balletgrl\>: More than hockey

\<MadFinn\>: Stop! Well, I dunno if I like him as much as I used to like him

\<Balletgrl\>: What r u talking about? U LOVE HIM

\<MadFinn\>: Aimee! I sort of like someone else now

\<Wetwinz\>: Who else is there?

\<Balletgrl\>: OMG Fiona Maddie likes ur brother Chet

\<MadFinn\>: Aimee! I do not like Chet ">(

\<Wetwinz\>: TGFT

\<Balletgrl\>: then WHOOOOOOO

\<MadFinn\>: well there's this guy next door I never knew he lived there but I think he just moved in last year and my parents were getting divorced then so I was probably a little spazzy and didn't notice him I don't know

\<Balletgrl\>: what's the dude's name?

<MadFinn>: he's a 9th grader @ FHJH
   and his name is Josh
<Wetwinz>: Josh Turner?
<MadFinn>: Do you know him?
<Balletgrl>: He's only the star of
   the hockey team, Maddie. Everyone
   knows Josh Turner.
<MadFinn>: I didn't know him
<Balletgrl>: I didn't know he lived
   in our neighborhood
<Wetwinz>: So y do u like HIM all
   of a sudden??
<MadFinn>: IDK
<Wetwinz>: But what about Hart?
<MadFinn>: that's exactly what Egg
   asked me--do u guys talk about
   EVERYTHING 2gether??
<Wetwinz>: maybe
<Balletgrl>: u know my brother is
   friends with Josh.
<MadFinn>: does the whole world know
   Josh except for me?
<Wetwinz>: LOL
<Balletgrl>: so what about
   Hart??????????
<MadFinn>: I haven't forgotten him
   DW!!
<Wetwinz>: it would be sooo cool
   to double-date I know I said
   that b4
<Balletgrl>: can't we triple-date?

<MadFinn>: yeah maybe YOU can go
   out with Chet

"Let's eat!" Gramma's voice called out from the kitchen, interrupting Maddie's chat.

Madison quickly signed off. Normally, she'd have wanted to stay online as long as possible, but tonight she felt more like spending time with her grandmother.

"I notice you haven't been as tired this afternoon," Gramma said. "Your spirits seem brighter."

"I do feel better," Madison said. "Thanks to you."

"Well, that's what Grammas are for."

"Maybe I can go to school on Monday?" Madison said.

"What about your cough?" Gramma said. "You know my rules."

Coughcoughcough.

Madison covered her mouth. Then her nose twitched.

Ahhhchooooo!

"How come I was feeling fine until you started talking about feeling fine?" Madison asked aloud. She shook off the sneeze. "Wait! Don't say it. Murphy's Law, right?"

"Exactly," Gramma said with a nod.

They finished dinner and dessert, but it was still

early in the evening. Madison wanted to watch a double feature on Pay-Per-View, but Gramma gave that idea a big thumbs-down.

"I want you to go to bed," Gramma said.

"Bed! No way! Gramma, I understand that you're worried about me and all that," Madison said. "But it's only eight-thirty and I'm twelve, not six. I don't have a bedtime like I used to."

Gramma shook her head. "Maddie . . ."

Without another word, an exasperated Madison and Phin headed upstairs, to make Gramma happy.

And it wasn't torture altogether, because, once her bedroom door was closed, Madison didn't sleep. Once again she powered up her computer. After she plugged in her super secret password, two special e-mails appeared in her mailbox.

```
From: ff_budgefilms
To: MadFinn
Subject: NONE
Date: Sat 27 Sept 4:20 PM
I miss you, honey bear. I feel
terrible leaving when you are sick.
I'll hurry home.

Love, Mom
```

Madison sighed. She missed Mom, too. Mom never made her go to bed that early.

The next e-mail was from her keypal.

From: Bigwheels
To: MadFinn
Subject: You Won't Believe This BUT
Date: Sat 27 Sept 5:14 PM

E-mails R contagious. I think that maybe I caught your flu. Isn't that what u have? I almost fainted yesterday so my dad took me to the doctor. My fever was 102 degrees. That is the highest fever I have ever had. What's the highest fever you've ever had? I had to come home and take a cold bath and get into bed. Today I don't have a fever anymore but I still feel weird because I threw up this morning. Ugh. I hate being sick so much. I don't think I'll have to go to school Monday though and THAT is a good thing.

Have u seen that boy next door again? I like his name. One of my friends at school is named Joshua. That's close. U still didn't tell me what happened 2 Hart? Is he still around? Write back soon. I have to go take a nap now.

Yours till the bath tubs,

Vicki aka Bigwheels

Madison wanted to write a response to Bigwheels right away. She needed to wish her a speedy recovery and tell her that she was sorry about Bigwheels's being sick, too.

But Madison stopped herself from hitting REPLY.

She couldn't write back yet. She didn't have an answer to a question that Bigwheels had been asking for a couple of days.

What *had* happened to Hart?

And what was Madison going to do about her *change* of heart?

Chapter 10

 Sickest

It's very, very, VERY early on a Monday and I am already up and dressed for school. I got so much sleep when I was sick (my brilliant theory) that I am wide awake (and feeling better) now. Meanwhile, Gramma is down in the kitchen and doesn't know I'm up here writing in a file. Sometimes it's fun being sneaky.

Fiona got sick again yesterday because her brother Chet came down with a fever, too. Bummer. But Aim is better and so am I (according to what the thermometer says which is 98.9 and my lack of cough). Thankfully I never had the throw-ups.

I am, however, not completely well. I still feel a little sick about boys. In fact, this may be the SICKEST I've been about one particular boy in a looooong time.

All I can think about is Josh Turner.

What will I REALLY do when I see him in person in the halls or in the lunchroom @ FHJH? Will he say hello and be nice or blow me off like I'm some puny, insignificant seventh grader? That could happen, right? I mean, I am just a seventh grader.

Wow. I hope not.

The right outfit is essential, as Aimee would say. Right now I am wearing a patchwork skirt and sweater top. The skirt is from the Boop-Dee-Doop outlet store that just opened. Stephanie got it for me. She said it makes me look taller. Josh is tall. And the sweater is purple so my eyes sparkle a little. At least I think they sparkle. I wonder if Josh will get close enough to see my eyes--or if he'll even care.

What do boys like him care about anyway?

Madison glanced at the clock and realized she needed to hurry. Aimee would be arriving to walk to school with her in a few minutes. But they'd be a twosome today—not a threesome. Since Fiona had had a relapse, she was staying home.

Madison was excited to get back to a normal

school—and life—schedule. So was Aimee. When she knocked on the door of the Finn house, Aimee couldn't stop yammering.

"I was thinking a lot about our optical illusions project, and I think we should have a home page that is like an illusion. You know, if you select one part of it, a page pops up, and if you select another part of it, another page pops up, and then there are different illusions on different pages, and the illusions can rotate and fly across the screen. . . ."

"Slow down, Aim," Madison said. "who's going to program all that?"

"I don't know," Aimee responded. "You?"

"Ha!" Madison let out a fake laugh. "I don't know how to make stuff fly across the screen. Anyway, didn't Lindsay say we have an extension on the project?"

"Yes," Aimee said. "So you don't want to talk about the project now. Is that it?"

"I just have my mind on other stuff. You know. . . ." Madison's voice drifted.

"On other stuff . . . but not Hart, though, right?" Aimee said.

"What is that supposed to mean?" Madison asked.

"Ever since you told me about that other guy at school . . ." Aimee rolled her eyes. "I just think that it's really weird that you could like Hart soooo much and then, all of a sudden, you don't like him—"

122

"I never said that I didn't like him anymore," Madison replied.

"Well, you're totally blowing him off," Aimee said.

"I am not!" Madison frowned. "Whose side are you on? Hart's or mine?" she asked.

Madison had a thing about taking sides. She liked to have as many people in her corner as possible. Just then, however, she felt like the cheese in Farmer in the Dell. She stood alone.

"Maddie, I'm on *your* side. Duh. Of course," Aimee said.

Madison smiled. They were at the front door of their school by then. "Thanks," she said.

"Let's meet up after third period," Aimee said, hugging Madison before they went their separate ways.

"Sure thing," Madison said. She slung her book bag over her shoulder and walked in the opposite direction, toward her science classroom.

Mr. Danehy's class was packed, even though the second bell had not yet rung. Madison scanned the room.

Poison Ivy sat on a stool by the lab table where she and Madison always sat. Despite their differences, they somehow managed to coexist as science partners in class.

At least, they tried to coexist.

"Could you share the lab assignments with me?"

Madison asked when she took her assigned seat at Ivy's left.

"What assignments are you talking about?" Ivy snapped.

"I missed a couple of labs and some homework when I was sick last week. . . ." Madison said.

Ivy held her hand up in front of her face like a shield. "So? And stay away from me. I don't want to get sick."

"I'm not sick anymore," Madison said.

"Whatever," Ivy said.

"Ivy, can I please read your notes? You *are* my partner," Madison insisted.

"You know I don't take notes," Ivy said. "I don't have to help you."

"Yes, you do. . . ." Madison sighed and gave up. She wanted to take Ivy's notebook and hurl it across the room . . . or better yet, take Ivy and hurl *her* across the room. But she took a deep breath instead.

On the other side of the room, Hart waved. Madison smiled back.

She could ask Hart for his notebook. Madison had never read anything Hart wrote down in class, but he did raise his hand a lot, and Madison assumed he was a strong science student. Egg teased him once with the nickname Smart Hart.

At the end of class, Madison decided to ask Mr. Danehy directly about makeup work. He handed

Madison copies of the previous week's lab on germs.

"Miss Finn, I appreciate your following up on this, but I really think you should work with another student, not just with me," Mr. Danehy said. "Why don't you talk to Nancy Powers? She's an excellent student. Or Beezie Webster? Or maybe Hart Jones?"

Madison gulped.

Hart? Her teacher was telling her to work on questions with Hart? What did that mean? Was that some kind of sign?

Once outside of the classroom, Madison raced to her locker. She had only a few moments to grab her books for history class. There was a quiz review on the American Revolution, and she didn't want to miss it.

"Madison?"

Madison turned to see who was saying her name. It was Josh Turner. In person.

"I thought that was you," Josh said. "I didn't recognize you without the windowpane. Uh . . . that's a joke. A bad joke, but who cares?"

"Oh," Madison said. Her tongue was officially tied.

"I hope you weren't freaked by those dumb signs the other night. I was just playing," Josh said, brushing the hair away from his face.

"Oh, that's okay," Madison said.

"Yeah, well . . . I have class. See you around," Josh said.

"See you through the window!" Madison chirped.

Josh laughed. "Sure."

Madison fanned herself with a notebook. She felt as though the blood had stopped pumping through her veins. Her whole body was in a state of quasi-shock. Josh looked even cuter walking away than he had up close.

See you around.

Madison turned back to lock her locker. But she wasn't alone.

"Finnster!"

Madison jumped. "Hart, you scared me."

"I was trying to say hello in science, but then class started and . . ."

"I was so focused on catching up on work I missed when I was sick. . . ." Madison said.

"Oh, that's okay," Hart said as he stuffed his hands in his pockets. "Um . . . was that Josh Turner you were just talking to?" he asked.

Madison nodded. "Yeah. He's my neighbor, you know."

"I know," Hart said. "I was there the other day on the porch."

"Of course," Madison said. "Look, can we talk later? I really have to run."

"Later?" Hart nodded. "No prob. Later."

But Madison didn't connect with Hart later. At lunch, even though Hart had an empty seat next to him at the regular orange table, Madison sat with

Lindsay. They talked girl talk, about Fiona's being sick again and about the failure of their Web project to get off the ground. The flu had them all seriously sidetracked. A few times during lunch, Madison glanced over at Hart, just to see if he were looking. But Hart just joked with Egg and the others as he did every day. He didn't look her way once.

"Are you going to say anything to him?" Lindsay whispered at the end of lunch.

"Who?" Madison asked.

"Maddie!" Lindsay smirked. She tilted her head in Hart's direction to indicate him without saying his name out loud. Madison pretended to ignore her.

Lindsay got the point and promised to shut up about Hart and other boys. On the way out of the cafeteria, however, as they headed up to the media lab, Lindsay broke her promise.

"Look!" Lindsay pointed down the hall. "It's the other one!"

Madison nudged Lindsay hard with her elbow. "Shhhhh!" Madison said. "Someone might hear you! I am so embarrassed."

Madison stared. Josh was standing there with a few friends. She watched as he walked down the hall. The truth was that Josh didn't really walk—he swaggered. His arms swung in perfect motion, like two alternating pendulums.

How had she never noticed him before? How had

this ninth grader been drifting around FHJH for the whole school year so far *and* living next door to Madison without their orbits crossing?

When Josh turned toward the gymnasium and student lounge, Madison and Lindsay veered off toward the media lab. They dumped their bags at a computer terminal in the back.

"Let's send Fiona an e-mail," Lindsay suggested. "I told her I would."

"Great idea!" Madison said.

Lindsay turned on the computer and logged on to the e-mail program.

```
From: LuvNstuff
To: Wetwinz
Subject: MORE GOSSIP 4 U
Date: Mon 29 Sept 1:02 PM
```
Fiona! Maddie & I are in the media lab @ school and we had to write. HOW ARE YOU? I can't believe Chet made u sick all over again. N e way I have major gossip

"Wait! Don't tell her about Josh," Madison said. "Or Hart. I really *don't* want to talk about boys."

"You don't want to talk about Josh? Why not?" Lindsay asked. "That's the juicy stuff. What's your problem?"

"Please," Madison insisted. "I know if we tell her anything she'll tell Egg. I just don't want everyone to know my secrets, especially not Egg. He's the world's biggest blabbermouth. . . ."

Madison felt bad keeping something hidden from one of her BFFs. But she was feeling confused enough about boys just then without gossip or rumors messing it up. Plus, she was worried about writing anything down on a school computer. What if someone who used the computer after her were to read what she wrote?

Lindsay's fingers froze over the keyboard. "Okay, so if I can't tell Fiona the best gossip about you, then what do I write?" she asked.

"Just tell her we're working on the optical illusions Web page."

"Fine," Lindsay said. She kept typing.

```
Madison and I were talking about
the optical illusions project. We
miss you lots.
```

"What else am I supposed to write about?" Lindsay asked.

"Just say . . . we found a few books . . . and a cool Web site," Madison suggested. "I don't know. Make something up. She won't know the difference."

Lindsay typed some more.

```
Have u done n e work on it yet?
Maddie sez she found a Web site but
I have to admit that I didn' t do
```

n e work and I'm the only one of us who isn't sick! It's a good thing there's an extension. E us l8r?

Lindsay signed the e-mail and hit SEND. "That was so lame," she said.

Feeling guilty about not having done any work, they took an hour to surf the Web for ideas. Madison had a little bit of a headache (a leftover from being sick), and she was still coughing, but it was fun to be back at school, working and hanging out with her friends.

Although they had agreed to meet Aimee up in the media lab during the free period, Aimee never showed up. Madison figured that Aimee had a dance meeting or a study hall she'd forgotten. Usually Fiona was a space case, but being sick was making all of them a little absentminded this week.

Lindsay plugged the words *optical illusion* into a search engine. It turned up brainteasers, checkerboard shadows, and various geometric designs. One picture showed the face of an old woman, which turned into an Eskimo in the blink of an eye. Many Web pages were devoted to M. C. Escher, an artist who drew, among other things, pictures of staircases that led nowhere. Another Web site was devoted entirely to shape and color illusions that quilters could use as patterns for their quilts.

There was more than enough for them to use there—the hard part would be figuring out what *not* to use. Lindsay and Madison each took notes for their Web page. Madison saved the Web addresses with art on them so she could find images to post later.

Gramma Helen was waiting up with dinner when Madison got home from school. The first thing Gramma did was reach out to touch Madison's forehead.

"Not too warm," Gramma said, hugging Madison. "And how's the cough?"

"It's still there," Madison said, groaning.

"I could have picked you up at school, you know," Gramma said.

"I know," Madison replied. "I needed to stay late to work on this Web project I'm doing with my friends."

"Your mother called," Gramma said.

"Is she coming home?" Madison asked.

"Tomorrow, I think," Gramma said. "She's calling back with the times of her flights and all that. I told her we were getting along famously. . . ."

"Of course!" Madison giggled. "Just the two of us and not all three of us, right?"

"Two's company. . . ."

"Three's a crowd!" Madison joked.

"Oh, by the way, I saw that boy next door again," Gramma said. "We walked the dogs together this afternoon. He's a nice boy. Phin loves his dog. I think

131

he said her name was Poodle or something like that."

"You know his dog's *name*?" Madison pulled off her jacket and threw her stuff down in the hallway. "You went for a walk with him?"

She stood there, her mouth wide open.

She prayed that Gramma Helen hadn't said anything embarrassing—like, "my granddaughter thinks you're super duper cute!"

Madison wondered why it wasn't *she* who had walked the dog that day. She knew the answer.

Murphy's Law.

"I made soup again tonight," Gramma said. "You don't mind, do you?"

Madison shook her head. She was in too much shock over Gramma's news to care about having soup for the umpteenth time already that week.

"I was thinking. Let's try some knitting tonight," Gramma suggested. "While you were at school today, I took a trip down to Far Hills Shoppes and got some yarn. You were always asking me to show you how to knit. We can make something for your mother. It's supposed to be a cold winter!"

Madison thought it was a good idea. Knitting was another way she could bond with Gramma. And it would be nice to make something for Mom.

Madison really missed Mom.

As she helped Gramma heat up the dinner, Madison's thoughts kept taking a wide detour. It was hard to think about knitting or homework or lasagna when she had Josh on the brain. She and he definitely had a connection . . . a spark . . . a *something*. Madison was sure of it.

She wondered if Josh would flash any signs in his window that night.

Chapter 11

Tuesday afternoon, after turning in to Blueberry Street on the walk home from school, Madison spotted Josh. He was way ahead of her, but Madison didn't think. She just started running.

"Hello!" Madison gasped when she caught up to him.

Josh whirled around. "Whoa. Hello, yourself. I didn't hear you."

Madison tried hard to keep from panting, but her mouth was dry from running so fast. She wiped her forehead and tried to look cool.

"Are you okay?" Josh asked. "You're purple."

"Oh, I have asthma," Madison said. It was a strange lie, but it sounded a lot better than, "Oh, I was just running to catch up to you."

"So, what's up?" Josh asked. He kept walking, and Madison could barely keep up with his pace after her long run. She wanted him to slow down so they would have time to talk before reaching their houses.

"What's up? Nothing much," Madison said, gulping air. "Don't you think it's funny how we never saw each other before last week?"

"Not really," Josh said. "I saw you a lot."

"You did?" Madison asked. She almost stopped in her tracks when he said that.

He really had noticed her. For a long time.

"Sure, I saw you," Josh said simply, staring straight ahead.

Madison checked her palms. They were definitely sweating.

She and Josh kept walking.

Josh told her about an upcoming hockey meet. Madison mentioned the class Web page project. They talked about the weather, dogs, and Principal Bernard's ugly ties.

We have so much in common, Madison thought happily. She caught herself staring up at Josh's round, brown eyes. He had longer eyelashes than Madison did.

"This is me," Josh said as they passed in front of his family's home. "See you around. I have to walk Cuddles."

"Who?"

"My poodle," Josh said.

Madison grinned. She wanted to say something smart or funny, but no words came out. Josh was halfway down the path to his front door before she managed to wave.

She was thinking so hard about Josh that Madison almost didn't notice Mom's briefcase in the front hall.

"Mom?" Madison cried out. "Are you home?"

Gramma appeared at the doorway to the kitchen, drying a bowl.

"She's not here," Gramma said.

"What? But her stuff is right here—" Madison cut herself off and sat down on the wooden chair in the hallway. "She couldn't wait to go out again? She knew I was coming home today to see her. . . ."

"I know," Gramma said, stroking the top of Madison's head. "I told her you would be upset. . . ."

"I can't believe this. . . ." Madison felt her eyes tear up.

"It's okay, Maddie—" Gramma tried to say.

"How?" Madison asked. "How is it okay?"

Gramma shook her head. "Maddie, I know you wish your mother could be here all the time for you. But your mother . . . she's got a lot to juggle. We have to be understanding of that."

"What are you talking about, Gramma? I heard you yelling at her."

"Yelling? No, I don't yell. We disagree sometimes. . . ."

"Loudly. You disagree *loudly*. Sounds like yelling to me," Madison said.

"Madison Finn, I don't appreciate your tone of voice," Gramma said. Her lips were pursed into a little round *O* that seemed to say, "Oh, don't you mess with me!"

Madison retreated. "I'm sorry, Gramma. I just don't think that—"

"What's going on here?" Mom's voice cut through the hallway tension.

"Mom!" Madison screeched. "You're home!"

"Of course I am," Mom said. "Mother, didn't you tell Maddie that I was back?"

"Yes," Gramma grumbled. "But then you walked right out again."

Mom sighed. "I walked right out? Mother, I went over to the main office to pick up the rough cut of the documentary, so we could have a private screening."

"I know," Gramma said. "I didn't have a chance to say anything yet."

Madison couldn't stay mad. She wanted to hug Mom too much. She threw her arms around Mom's waist and squeezed her tightly.

"You're so strong," Mom gasped. She bent down to hug Madison right back. "How are you feeling?"

"She went to school today—" Gramma started to report.

Madison interrupted. "I'm feeling better now that you're home, Mom."

137

Mom pulled a videotape with the rough cut of the film out of a small tote. She directed everyone, including Phin, in to the family room. Gramma, Madison, and the dog parked themselves in front of the TV set.

"I should really get dinner going," Gramma said. "You two can watch together without me."

"Mother . . ." Mom said sternly as she popped in the tape.

Gramma threw her up hands. "Fine, fine," she said, sitting back down. "I'll watch. We'll all watch."

Mom was like a fleece blanket. Madison was instantly warmed by her presence in the house. Madison had missed Mom more than she had been willing to admit.

The gears of the machine stuck, so the tape didn't play right away. While Mom fiddled with the controls to get things started, Madison tickled Phin's belly.

Gramma tapped her fingers on the arm of the chair.

"I really should get the food started," Gramma said, starting up.

"Mother! I want you to see this," Mom replied. "We can get dinner later."

Once again, Gramma sat back down and stopped talking.

The tape finally rolled.

Madison had seen almost all of the documentary work Mom had ever done. A profile of sea turtles

138

called *Underwater Magic* was Madison's personal favorite. But Gramma Helen had not seen much of Mom's work. Her excuse was that she didn't really "understand" what Mom did. Mom's reply was always, "What's to understand? I make little movies about real things."

This time, Gramma Helen didn't have a choice. She was watching.

The screen was filled with white light. Then a series of dots started to appear, one by one, until the entire screen was blacked out. Burning through the black came luminous white letters that read: *Blackout: AIDS Around the Globe.*

Gramma crossed her legs. Madison couldn't even tell if Gramma were really looking at the screen.

Mom's documentary focused mostly on AIDS in Africa. In it were interviews with families suffering from the disease. She showed communities five years earlier as compared to the present day. Some places were losing as much as fifty percent of their populations. Alongside the photos and live footage of people, Mom explained, she would be cutting in statistics that would flash on the screen.

Slowly, frame by frame, as the movie proceeded, Madison noticed that Gramma was starting to pay more and more attention to it. About twenty minutes into *Blackout*, Gramma seemed one hundred percent focused. She even seemed a little teary during certain parts.

"Frannie, this is astounding," Gramma said, after a segment that featured a young boy of twelve who was bringing up his two brothers alone after all of the other members of his family had contracted and died from AIDS.

"What am I complaining about?" Madison said aloud. "I've got a little cough and I think I'm sick?"

"Well, honey bear," Mom said. "You don't have to compare yourself to these people. Your situation is a lot different. You were sick, too."

By that point, Gramma couldn't take her eyes from the TV screen.

"Frannie, this is remarkable. I had no idea you made such important films," Gramma said. "I'm astounded."

Mom just smiled. "I think this one has a chance to make a difference."

"Frannie, I just don't know what to say. . . ." Gramma said.

"Don't say anything," Mom said. She went over to her mother and squeezed in right next to her on the chair. "Mother, you always know the right thing to say. It's me who has trouble communicating with you."

Madison wrinkled her brow. *What was going on?* They weren't talking about the film anymore.

"Oh, Frannie," Gramma wiped a tear from her eye. "Frannie, I'm so . . . *proud*."

"Mother," Mom said. She was crying a little, too.

"Um . . . Mom? Gramma? Are you okay?" Madison asked. "Did I miss something?"

Madison had a hunch that Mom and Gramma were crying because they had been arguing all week long and now it was make-up time, but she couldn't be sure. She glanced around the room and through the window. The weather had gotten cooler since she'd come home from school. She could see the trees blowing.

As Mom and Gramma continued to talk, Madison stood up and looked out the window. Other kids were coming home from school, riding bikes in the road and chasing each other from yard to yard. She could see them all as they passed by the Finns' front porch.

And then Josh Turner walked by.

It looked like as though he were standing outside the Finn house, looking in. He rocked from foot to foot, staring straight ahead.

Was he spying on Madison?

Once she saw him, Madison's heart began pounding.

"I'll be back," Madison declared, walking to the door.

"Have you seen enough of the film?" Mom said with a wink. "Where are you going?"

"Out," Madison said. Her eyes darted around the room. *What was she going out for?* "To walk the dog!" Madison said when her eyes landed on Phin.

"Okay," Mom said. "We'll be right here."

Gramma sniffled. "Right here," she said as she squeezed Mom's hand.

Madison raced out of the family room, up the stairs, and into her closet. She grabbed a jean jacket and her sunglasses. Phin danced around in little circles when he realized that it was time to go outside for a walk. Madison clipped on his collar and leash and headed for the front door.

As she stepped onto the porch, Madison saw what Josh was staring at and it wasn't Madison's house. He was outside helping his dad trim the hedges and clean up the yard.

"Hey!" Madison called out. She hustled over to where Josh was standing.

He looked at her for a moment without saying anything.

"I saw you. . . . and thought I would . . . come out and say hello. . . ." Madison said. She bobbed her head and smiled her widest smile. She knew the jacket she was wearing brought out the color in her cheeks. She wanted Josh to notice.

"Hey," Josh said quietly.

He's dumbfounded. He doesn't know what to say.

"So, you're helping clean up the yard?" Madison asked.

He's staring at me.

"Yeah, I'm kinda busy. . . ." Josh replied.

Phin yanked at the leash and Madison almost lost her balance.

"Whoops!" Madison said, recovering.

Josh stifled a giggle.

He thinks I'm cute.

Madison cast her eyes down toward the sidewalk. *How did Aimee flirt?* Madison tried to remember. *She bats her eyelashes a lot.* Madison did the same.

"Are you okay?" Josh asked a moment later.

"Me? Of course," Madison said.

"Because you . . . well . . . is there something in your eye?" Josh asked.

He noticed.

"Nothing's *wrong*, no," Madison said. She couldn't take her eyes off Josh.

"Cute dog," Josh said.

"His name is Phinnie. Where's your dog?" Madison asked. She was about to ask if they could walk their dogs together, but then she chickened out. She wanted him to ask her, anyway.

"Look, I really have to go . . . uh . . . help my dad," Josh said, pulling back with a wave. "See you around."

Madison stood there with Phin and watched Josh walk back into his own house. He gave Madison one last little wave from his top step.

After he'd disappeared, she walked Phinnie down the block so he could get more fresh air—and so she could take a few deep breaths herself. It felt good not to be sick anymore. The cough still lingered, but she could breathe easier than she'd been able to in a week.

Josh is so great.

Phin sniffed at every bush and mailbox. They didn't get back home for half an hour. By the time Madison returned, she found Gramma and Mom in the kitchen preparing dinner together.

No one argued at the dinner table as they had before Mom's trip. Madison was relieved. In fact, now it seemed as if Mom and Gramma were having *fun* together. After supper, Mom didn't retreat to her office to work as she usually did. Instead, she and Gramma just sat in the living room talking.

Madison headed upstairs to her room. She couldn't wait to look through her bedroom window over at Josh's window.

It was dark outside by now. The light was off in his room.

Madison curled up on her window seat with her laptop and waited for him to go into his room and turn on the light. While she waited, she opened up the notebook for their optical illusions project. Madison had to format a dummy Web page. Aimee could provide the images later.

Next, Madison began typing on her laptop.

```
Show a grid with black squares and
white lines. When you look at the
grid, you see invisible black dots.

Show cube drawn w/lines and 1 side
```

shaded in--is it the front or back
that's shaded? Looks like both.
Show weird rotating spiral and if
you stare at it for too long and
then look @ your hand, it looks
like bugs are crawling under your
skin!!!!!!

Madison kept glancing over at Josh's house.
Finally, a light went on in his room. She saw a
shadow and then Josh himself, standing in the window. Madison put her laptop on the floor and stood
up to wave. She had a sign already made.

HOW R U?

Josh stood motionless in the window across the
way. Madison thought he was looking in her direction, but she couldn't be positive.

HOW R U?

She pushed her sign up to the glass and waited.

All at once, Josh pulled the curtain across his window. The light went out again.

"Wait!" Madison cried out, even though Josh
couldn't hear her or see her anymore. She slumped
down on to the window seat and ripped up her
sign.

Sometimes, when Madison felt embarrassed, she
could sense her cheeks getting red or her hands getting hot. But right now, her entire body was flushed.
She couldn't speak or move for a few seconds.

Phin, who'd curled up next to Madison's monkey slippers on the floor, looked up when he heard Madison start mumbling to herself.

She leaned down, retrieved her laptop, and opened another file.

 Josh

He saw me. I know he did. He looked right over into my room just like all the other times.

I know. Someone called for him so he got distracted. Or maybe he suddenly remembered a phone call he needed to make. Or what if his dog yanked at his pant leg? Or maybe he really couldn't see anything in my room. I didn't have my bright lamp or my overhead light on. That was dumb of me. I wish I had his phone number so I could call and apologize for him not being able to see. I am sure he was looking forward to talking as much as I was.

Knock-knock.

"Can I come in, Maddie?" Gramma whispered through the door.

"Yeah, Gramma," Madison cried back. "Come on in."

"I just wanted to say good night and sleep tight," Gramma said. "Since it's my last night staying with you."

"I can't believe you have to leave so soon," Madison said.

"Well, it's been a week," Gramma said. "And I need to get back to Mabel and my other friends. They've been holding my seat at the bingo hall."

"Thanks for everything," Madison said.

"Thank you, too," Gramma said. "I hope that my being here helped you to get well just a little bit faster."

"Oh, it did! It did," Madison said. "Especially the soup. And the soup. Oh, yeah, and the soup."

They both laughed.

"Gramma?"

"Yes."

"Do you remember what we talked about the other night?" Madison asked.

"About boys?" Gramma said with a wink.

"Do you think I'll ever fall in love, Gramma?"

"Love? Oh, Maddie, of course. You're only twelve. My goodness."

"I know it's silly, but I just wonder how you know."

"How you know when you're in love, you mean?" Gramma asked.

Madison nodded. "Dad tried to explain it to me when he married Stephanie, but that's Dad, and he's a guy, and he doesn't understand what it's like to be a girl. And Mom always tells me that I should just be patient, but sometimes it's so hard to do that. Why can't it happen for me?"

"Well, I can see you've given this some thought," Gramma said.

"I want to be in love," Madison admitted. "And I think I've found the right guy."

"Well," Gramma said. "I'd say you have all the guys in the world after you. But that's because you're my granddaughter, and I think you're perfect. Just think about those young boys who came to see you when you were sick!"

"Oh, Gramma, those are just friends."

"You never know," Gramma said. "Sometimes love is waiting just outside your own backyard."

Madison grinned. Once again, Gramma had said *exactly* the right thing.

Chapter 12

Madison poured pancake batter into the pan and watched as half of it was spit back onto the stove.

"I can't do this!" she cried, nearly tipping over a bowl of eggs.

"Yes, you can. Just make smaller pancakes," Gramma advised, helping Madison to clean up the mess.

Mom put on a pot of coffee and turned up the sound on the CD player in the kitchen. She danced around to a song called "Celebrate."

Indeed, they were celebrating Gramma's last day with an honorary "Thank You for Coming All the Way from Chicago to Help Madison Get Well Soon" breakfast. On the menu was Gramma's favorite: banana pancakes with sliced strawberries on top.

149

Phin loved all the activity in the kitchen, mostly because he got the extra scraps that fell from the counter, and because he liked dancing around everyone else's busy feet.

"I have to go to school soon," Madison said. "I don't want you to go," she told Gramma.

Gramma gave her a hug. "Oh, sure you do," she said with a hint of sadness in her voice. "Remember what we said? Two's company, but three's a crowd?"

"Not with you here, Gramma. Not really."

"I'll write you a note, Maddie, if you're late, but hurry it up," Mom said.

Mom hardly ever made excuses for Madison to be late or to miss days of school. But since returning from her business trip, it seemed as though Mom had a new perspective. Madison even noticed Mom smiling more.

Through the kitchen window, Madison caught a glimpse of Josh leaving his house. She was tempted to dash out the front door and hurry after him. But she couldn't. This was Gramma's last morning.

Besides, Madison didn't want Josh to get scared off by all of her attention. She was determined to play it cooler than cool today. He would figure out her true feelings slowly, over time. That was the plan.

"These pancakes are *deeelicious*!" Gramma exclaimed as she took her first bite. "Thank you for breakfast, Maddie."

Madison and Gramma sat together at the table for a few more minutes before Mom pointed at the clock.

"It's after eight, Maddie," Mom said. "It's okay to be a little late for homeroom, but I don't want you missing classes."

Madison nodded and grabbed her orange bag. The weather outside had warmed up again, so she wore cotton pants, a T-shirt, and flip-flops with little flowers on them. There was nothing like a bonus summer day in the fall.

Gramma promised Madison she would send more e-mails. She would come to visit Far Hills again very soon, too, especially since her bad hip hadn't bothered her once.

Madison kissed Gramma good-bye for the fifth time. "Don't forget your vaporizer and your saltwater gargler. You left them in the upstairs bathroom," Madison reminded her.

Mom grabbed the car keys. "Let's go!" she said.

They dashed out of the house and into the car.

"I love you, Gramma Helen!" Madison cried as they pulled out of the driveway.

Phin stood on the top step of the porch, barking his head off.

Madison agreed to meet her BFFs (minus Fiona, who was still home sick) in the lunchroom around noon on Wednesday. While Aimee grabbed her usual yogurt and plain toast, Lindsay grabbed a plate of hot macaroni and cheese and put it onto her tray. Meanwhile, Madison stood by the school salad bar picking through the chopped vegetables, lettuce, and fruits, nuts, and salad dressings.

As they turned in to the main room of the cafeteria to sit down, Madison spotted Josh and his friends. She felt herself pulled to him as if by some magnetic force. She told her friends to go ahead, and pretended to go for another item at the salad bar.

"Hey, Finnster!"

Wham! Just like that, Hart cut right into Madison's path, blocking her view of Josh and the rest of the lunchroom.

"Are you going to sit down with everyone?" Hart asked.

"Sit down?" Madison said, shuffling along with Hart while trying to keep Josh in her line of vision.

"Yes," Hart said. He stopped walking, so Madison stopped, too. "I wanted to talk to you about the seventh grade Web project. . . ."

Madison realized that they'd stopped right in front of Poison Ivy's table.

Ivy and the drones looked up at Madison with nostrils flared.

"Um . . ." Madison asked, nudging Hart toward another table on the other side of the cafeteria aisle. "Can we talk at the table?"

Hart nodded. "Okay, sure."

"Oh, hi, Hart. Do you want to sit? You can sit down here," Ivy said. "There's plenty of room for you."

Madison waited for Hart to respond. He often sat with the enemy instead of with the rest of Madison's friends. But today, Hart walked away without even acknowledging Ivy's presence.

Madison was dumbfounded.

So was Ivy.

It was difficult for Madison not to laugh—hard—in her face. But she restrained herself, even as Ivy flipped her hair and tried to act as if nothing had happened.

As Madison followed Hart, she refocused her eyes on the back of the room. Where was Josh sitting? Was he still in the cafeteria? She couldn't spot him in the room.

"So, I was wondering if maybe you wanted to team up and do some extra-credit work in Mr. Danehy's class," Hart said. "I didn't know if you knew about his offer or not, since you were out sick."

"Uh-huh," Madison mumbled, distracted.

"Did he tell you about it?" Hart asked.

"Uh-huh," Madison said.

"I know most people are going to do it with their lab partners, but since you and Ivy aren't exactly friends—"

"What are you talking about?" Madison asked blankly.

153

"Science class," Hart said.

"I have a lab partner," Madison said.

"Yeah, I know, but, like I just said . . ."

Before Hart could finish his thought, the two of them reached their regular seats at the orange table at the back of the room. Egg and Dan were sitting there talking to Aimee and Lindsay—boys on one end, girls on the other. Chet, Fiona, and Drew were all out sick.

Aimee looked up and saw Madison approaching with Hart. She made a funny smiley face. "Hey, Maddie," she said. "What are you and Hart talking about?"

Hart slid into a chair next to Egg. He looked very confused.

"Seriously," Aimee whispered to her. "What is up with you two?"

"Yeah," Lindsay said. "Is something going on?"

Madison shook her head. "He just wanted to know if I'd do some science classwork with him."

"Wait! That's means something. Maddie, doesn't that mean something?" Lindsay asked.

"No, it doesn't mean anything," Madison said.

The three of them looked over at Hart, who was talking to Egg and Dan. He didn't look back at them.

"He is cute," Lindsay said. "I think you would make a nice couple."

"Jeez, Lindsay! Why don't you just announce it over the loudspeaker?" Madison cried.

"Sorry," Lindsay said.

"Where's that Josh guy today?" Aimee asked.

Madison shrugged. "He was here. I thought maybe we'd talk at lunch. Oh, well. I think he left."

"Ninth graders are so full of themselves," Aimee declared.

Lindsay and Madison nodded in agreement.

After school, Lindsay had to go to her piano lesson. Aimee and Madison decided to pay Fiona a visit. They called ahead of time to make sure Mr. and Mrs. Waters didn't mind visitors when both of their kids were home sick.

As they approached the Waterses' house, Madison got a squirmy feeling in her stomach. She wasn't sure if it was butterflies from her crush on Josh—or something she'd eaten at lunch. She tried to ignore the feeling.

They climbed the porch steps and rang the door-bell. Mr. Waters answered the door. He was wearing an apron—Mrs. Waters's apron. Aimee giggled when she saw him.

"Hello, girls!" he said with a wide smile. "I was just in the middle of baking a chicken casserole. Come on in."

Madison and Aimee waited for Fiona. She came down the stairs in her bathrobe and slippers, coughing.

"Fiona!" Madison cried when she saw her friend.

"I can't believe you're still sick. That totally stinks."

"We brought you a present," Aimee said, presenting Fiona with a Deep Purple Jawbreaker, Fiona's favorite candy.

"Aw, thanks," Fiona said, sniffling. "I miss you guys."

From behind the staircase, Madison heard the rumble of footsteps. Someone was coming up from the basement.

Fiona rolled her eyes. "My brother is being a real jerk," she said.

Chet appeared, carrying a tray of snacks. Behind him were Dan and Hart.

Dan nodded in the girls' direction. "What's up?"

"Hey, Aim. Hey, Finnster," Hart said.

Madison and Aimee said their hellos, and then the boys and girls parted ways. Fiona dragged her friends into the kitchen.

"Don't mind me!" Mr. Waters said as he carried a tray over to the stove. "Fix your friends a snack, Fiona," he added, walking out of the room again.

The girls sat down at the table and picked at a bowl of cheese popcorn.

"Did you see Josh today at school?" Fiona asked Madison.

Madison smirked. "Yes. I did."

Aimee hit Madison in the shoulder. "I can't believe you like someone who is practically in high school."

"I can't believe he lived next door to me all this time and I never met him—or even noticed him before now," Madison said. "It's like this lightbulb went off in my head."

"So what did he say when you talked the last time?" Fiona asked. "Tell me all the details. Is he going to ask you out?"

"Well." Madison put her finger up to her chin to indicate that she was thinking hard about the question. "He was outside in his yard, and I was walking Phinnie. . . ."

"Did he pet Phin? That's always a good sign," Aimee said. "The guy you like has to like your dog."

"What?" Madison asked. Then she giggled.

"Did you flirt with him?" Fiona asked.

"I think so," Madison said. "You know me. I'm not always that good at flirting."

Coughcoughcough.

Chet burst into the kitchen with his hand on his chest.

"Coming through!" he screeched. "Sick person! Take cover!"

Hart followed behind him, cracking up.

"Excuse us!" Chet snorted, making his way to the sink for a glass of water.

"You're disgusting!" Fiona yelled at him. "And totally rude!"

"Watch out, or she'll blow her nose on you!" Chet said.

Hart laughed. He looked over at Madison and smiled.

Madison smiled back.

"Let's go up to my room," Fiona said, glaring at her twin brother. "We'll leave rude boy down here while we work on our Web project."

"Actually, I have to go," Aimee said. "I have to meet my mom. She's taking me to a dance class tonight. I almost forgot about it."

"But we have to work on the optical illusions page," Madison said. "Wasn't that the reason we came over to see Fiona?"

"We can work on it later, can't we?" Fiona suggested.

Madison groaned. "We have barely done anything on it."

"I promise we'll work on it later," Aimee insisted.

Madison threw up her hands. "Fine. E me later."

Aimee grabbed her bag and scooted out of the kitchen to the front door.

"What are you doing for your project?" Hart asked.

Madison was about to tell him when Fiona interrupted.

"It's a secret!" Fiona said. "You'll see our amazing project at school just like everyone else." She didn't want Chet to know what she was doing, because she knew he'd find some way to sabotage her or the Web page. He always did.

"You're such a loser, Fiona," Chet grunted. He pushed Hart toward the kitchen door, and the boys went to find Dan. They'd left him downstairs in the basement by the new family computer.

"You and your brother make me laugh," Madison said when the boys were gone.

"I'm glad someone thinks it's funny," Fiona said.

The two girlfriends headed to Fiona's room with root beers in hand. Fiona's bed was unmade. Clothes were piled in one corner. A spread of teen magazines covered the floor.

"Nice! You have the latest issue of *Stylegirl*!" Madison said. She dropped to the floor and flipped through the pages.

"I have all the latest magazines," Fiona said. "Mom got them for me. I like to read when I'm sick, don't you? I take all the love quizzes and stuff. Hey! There's one magazine that has a quiz about finding your true mate. You should take it."

Madison laughed when she saw the headline of the quiz: TWO'S COMPANY, BUT THREE'S A CROWD: HOW DO YOU CHOOSE WHEN YOU LIKE *TWO*?

She stretched out on Fiona's floor, pen in hand.
Knock-knock.

"Who is it?" Fiona snapped. She opened the door, expecting to see her brother. But it wasn't Chet. Hart was standing there.

"Chet asked me to get a disk from you," Hart said.

"Oh," Fiona said. She grabbed a disk off her desk. "Fine. Here. Give it to him. And maybe then you guys can stop following us, okay?"

Hart shrugged. "Okay," he said.

Fiona shut the door right in Hart's face. She turned around and smiled.

"I think maybe it's a good idea if you're going out with that older guy," Fiona said. "Guys our age can be such dorks. Well, except for Egg, of course."

Madison grinned back at her BFF.

Going out with that older guy.

She liked the sound of that.

Chapter 13

When Madison arrived home from Fiona's, the Finn house was quiet—until Phinnie came scuttling around a corner, his little nails going *click-clack* on the hall floor.

"Rowooorrrroooooooo!" Phin howled. He jumped at Madison. Madison grabbed him in her arms.

"Hello?" Madison called out. No one rushed to the door with an offer of a hug or a bowl of soup. Gramma was long gone.

"Hi, Maddie," Mom responded.

With Mom back at home, the dinner plan was take-out.

"How was your day?" Mom asked.

"Okay, I guess," Madison said. "Aim and I went

over to see if Fiona was feeling better. I have a lot of homework tonight."

"It seems strange without Gramma here, doesn't it?" Mom said.

Madison nodded. "I liked having her here," she said. "But you know what? I like having you here, too. I like it when it's just us."

Mom kissed Madison on the top of her head. "Me, too," she said. She presented Madison with a Chinese take-out menu. "Pick something out for dinner tonight," she said.

Madison grabbed the menu and sat down on the staircase to read it. She knew one thing for sure. She wasn't ordering soup.

By the time the Chinese food delivery man brought the bag of Chicken with Cashews and Vegetable Surprise, with an extra-large order of brown rice, Madison and Mom were starved. They sat down at the kitchen table and laughed as they ripped open the bag of food.

"Here we are again!" Mom cheered as she poured them each a glass of ice water. She tossed a crunchy noodle to Phin, who poked it around on the floor with his little pug nose.

Madison grabbed her fortune cookie after they'd finished eating. She was hoping for some profound fortune like *Love is near* or *Love is all around you.*

She didn't know what to think when her fortune

cookie had no fortune in it at all. Madison wished she got fortunes like the ones Gramma got before coming to Far Hills.

While Mom was cleaning up the dinner dishes, Dad called.

"I'm back from my business trip!" he cried into the receiver. "Want to go out for dinner?"

"It's after seven, Dad," Madison sighed. "And Mom and I just finished dinner."

"No! Well, how about tomorrow, then?" Dad asked.

Madison held her hand over the receiver.

"Mom, it's Dad," she whispered. "Can I have dinner with him tomorrow?"

Mom nodded. "Of course," she said. "Maybe you can spend the night at his place. He can drive you to school from the apartment."

Madison liked that idea. So did Dad. They made a plan to meet the next evening at around six. Stephanie would make a Tex-Mex feast. That was one good thing about having a stepmother from Texas.

"You haven't told me how you're feeling, sweetheart," Dad said, sounding concerned.

"Oh, I got the flowers. Thanks. And I'm much better now. Still have the cough a little. The doctor said bronchitis takes a long time to go away."

"Wait!" Dad said. "I just got an idea. Why don't I come over there right now and take you out for dessert?"

"Right now? Dessert?" Madison asked. She glanced over at Mom and then whispered into the phone. "Dad, it's a school night."

"We'll grab a quick ice cream. It's a warm night."

"Well, I did get gypped on my Chinese fortune cookie. . . ." Madison said. "Let me ask Mom."

"He wants to take you for ice cream on a Wednesday night?" was Mom's response. "Is he kidding?"

Madison put on her best pleading face.

Mom sighed. "Okay," she finally said. "It's one of the last warm days."

Madison squealed and told Dad the good news. He agreed to come over right away. They would go downtown to everyone's favorite ice-cream joint, Freeze Palace.

Dad honked the horn when he arrived, and Madison ran outside and jumped in. Unfortunately, by the time they got to Freeze Palace and parked the car, it had started to rain. In a matter of moments, rain was coming down hard. It was only a quick summer rain, but people who'd been enjoying the warm evening got soaked.

Madison and Dad ducked into Freeze Palace to find a crowd of ice-cream eaters who'd been caught in the rain.

"Oh—I'm—soaked—" Madison said as they looked around.

Dad was focused on the menu. "Do you want

164

butternut crunch or chocolate chip?" he asked. He was getting his favorite, mint chip. They didn't have Madison's favorite, Cherry Ripple.

All of a sudden, Madison caught her breath.

A bunch of customers who'd been caught in the downpour stood nearby talking. In the middle of the group was a familiar face.

Josh Turner.

Madison left Dad at the counter and walked over toward Josh.

He recognized her immediately. "Hi, Madison."

"Hey, Josh," Madison said, worrying about whether or not her hair looked good.

"Wild night," he said. "I'm just here with a few friends. We were studying together for a test, but we snuck out to the movies."

Madison sighed. She imagined herself at the movies with Josh and his friends. She'd never been on a real movie date, but Madison liked to dream about what could happen on such a date, all alone in the dark.

Josh would reach his arm around her back and pull her closer to him.

He'd lean over and take her hand in his.

He'd move in for one . . . slow . . . kiss. . . .

"Madison?" Josh was trying to get Madison's attention. "What are *you* doing here?"

Madison pointed to Dad. "I'm with him. That's my dad."

Madison wanted to turn three shades of purple.
I'm with my dad.

It sounded so *seventh grade*.

"Oh," Josh said. "I recognize your dad from the neighborhood. He's always mowing the lawn the same time as my dad."

"Are you getting something?" Madison asked.

"Yeah, a cone," Josh replied. "Are you?"

"Oh, yes. . . ." Madison glanced at the glass display case. "A chocolate-chip cone," she said.

"No kidding! That's my favorite flavor," Josh said.

Madison swooned. "Really?" she said.

A girl with wet hair walked up to them and grabbed Josh's elbow.

"Did you order already?" the girl asked.

"Hey, Madison, this is Remy," Josh said.

Madison felt like she'd swallowed a fork.

Remy?

"Hi," Remy said in a soft voice. She had long, curly, black hair that was all frizzed out from the rain. Her clothes were wet, too. "I just got soaked outside," she said, pointing at her sneakers, which were completely drenched.

Madison looked down and then back up again at the two of them. She noticed that Josh had his hand on the small of Remy's back.

She felt as though someone had hit her with a stun gun.

Where had Remy come from?

As if the whole scene couldn't be made any worse, at that exact moment Dad walked over with their ice-cream cones.

"Maddie? It's late, honey. Can you talk to your friends another time?"

Dad gave Madison the perfect "out." But she couldn't move. Her feet were stuck to the linoleum floor.

She had officially put the freeze back into Freeze Palace.

Fortunately, the paralysis was fleeting. As soon as Madison regained control of her limbs, she grabbed Dad's arm and pulled him away.

She would eat her ice cream at home.

No good-byes for Josh or Remy.

Just a very quick escape.

On the drive home, Madison fought back a flood of tears.

After she had filled him in, Dad tried to be understanding. He made Madison feel a little less embarrassed about what had happened by telling her at least a hundred times that she was terrific. By the ninety-ninth time, she actually believed him.

Mom was even more consoling when Madison got home. Mom told her she was terrific, too.

Once her head stopped spinning, Madison headed upstairs to get ready for bed. She wasn't sure she could ever face Josh again after what had happened. And what would she tell her BFFs? She'd made such a big deal about the new guy, the ninth grader, the cool next-door neighbor she'd never noticed before.

Now what?

Madison logged onto her laptop.

An e-mail from Bigwheels popped right up. There was one from Gramma, too. Madison read them in order.

From: Bigwheels
To: MadFinn
Subject: I'm Better How About U
Date: Wed 1 Oct 6:11 PM

I haven't heard from you in a little while. Are you sick again? I'm better now. But I gave my flu to my little brother and sister so now almost everyone in the house is coughing. Oh well.

Remember that guy I sort of liked, Reggie? Well he e-mailed me and now I think I like him again. We were sort of going out except that we hadn't really gone anywhere yet. Do you think I could ask him out? Would that be weird? I know girls rule and all that but I still feel embarrassed about asking him. I want him to ask me. Is that wrong?

BTW: We just found out at the vet that Sparkles is having kittens! I am so excited I want to keep them all. My mom just laughed at me when I said that. "Maybe one," she said. LOL.

Write back! You haven't said anything about Josh and I want to hear all the juicy details, ok? I think it would be soooo cool if you guys fell in love and lived happily ever after.

Yours till the teddy bears,

Vicki aka Bigwheels

Gramma's e-mail was short and sweet.

From: GoGramma
To: MadFinn
Subject: Back Home
Date: Wed 1 Oct 7:03 PM
Home safe. But the house feels so empty with just me. I miss you already.

Hope you are feeling like your old

self again. Stay as fit as a fiddle.

Love, Gramma

Reading Gramma's kind e-mail made Madison wish that Gramma were still in Far Hills so she could tell her all about the Josh disaster.

Madison opened a new file.

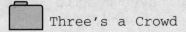 Three's a Crowd

Is this the face of permanent embarrassment? My cheeks will never be a normal color again. Help.

Rude Awakening: I thought having the flu was bad. But now I'm heartsick and there's no good medicine for that.

When I saw Josh with his girlfriend at Freeze Palace I thought I would shrivel up and die right there. Thank goodness none of my other friends were around. Egg would never have let me forget it.

How could I have been so wrong about him? Why did he write me those signs if he didn't like me? Why did he talk to me in school if he didn't want to get to know me better? He didn't want to go out with me, a lowly seventh grader. He already had a ninth-grade girlfriend. And what kind of a name is Remy anyway?

Is it my fate to be loveless? I don't get fortunes in my cookies. And I don't get the guy.

I feel sick all over again.

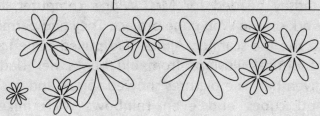

Chapter 14

By Thursday morning, Madison had recovered. She got up and got dressed, determined to face the world with a smile. At least that was what she told herself in the mirror.

"Look good, and feel good," Madison said to her reflection as she applied some strawberry-kiwi lip gloss. She wore her favorite T-shirt, faded Capri jeans, and clogs. Mom came into the bathroom and French-braided her hair with a ribbon. Madison put on the moonstone earrings Dad had given her and a silver ring on every finger. Lately she hadn't been wearing her rings that much. Today she wanted to have on as much armor as possible.

"Wow! You look so pretty today," Aimee said at

the lockers later in the morning, after homeroom class.

Madison smiled. She looked good. She felt good.

During study period, Madison, Aimee, Fiona, and Lindsay headed for Mrs. Wing's computer lab to work on the Web page project. They had permission to use the scanner. Aimee had pulled some images of optical illusions from old books her Dad had given her. The pictures showed spirals and curlicues and cubes and even rainbows with mixed-up colors. The girls needed to put all of it on a disk so Madison could start formatting the page over the weekend.

After a rocky start organizing the project, Madison, Aimee, Fiona, and Lindsay were now gaining momentum.

Lindsay had a great idea for the opening screen of the Web page. It would be a greeting that played a trick on the eyes. It was shaped like a road sign.

DO YOU
LOVE TO
SEE OPTICAL
ILLUSIONS ON THE
THE INTERNET?

They showed the illusion to Mrs. Wing. She didn't figure it out for at least a minute. Then she spotted the word *the* written twice. Madison loved the fact that they could fool a teacher, even if it was only for a short time.

After finishing up in the computer lab, Madison headed into the hallway with her friends.

"Look!" Aimee said. "It's Josh Turner."

Sure enough, Josh was standing in the hall, by the lockers. He was alone.

"Go talk to him," Fiona said, nudging Madison. "He's so cute."

"We'll wait here," Lindsay said.

Madison didn't budge. "I don't think so," she said. "Not right now."

"But you look so great," Aimee said. "You have to let him see you like this. He will ask you out in five seconds. Trust me."

Madison shook her head. "I don't think so," she said, slumping.

Brrrrrring.

The bell rang for the next class period. Josh disappeared down the hall in the opposite direction. Madison was relieved.

"Now you missed your chance!" Fiona said.

"Can we meet up later to finish scanning stuff?" Aimee asked. "I have to return some of these books to my dad tonight."

Lindsay nodded. "I can stay after school."

"Me, too," Madison said.

Fiona was the only one who had to go home. She

was still taking medicine for her lingering flu. "I'll help more tomorrow," she said.

Everyone was fine with that.

"Even if we can't always be here working together, we're making progress," Madison said. "That's good, right?"

"Good?" Aimee scoffed. "Our project is going to kick some major butt."

Fiona and Lindsay laughed, grabbed their book bags, and ran off to the next class. Madison needed to get something out of her locker, so Aimee waited with her.

"Is something wrong?" Aimee asked.

The halls were starting to clear out. The second bell was about to ring.

"I'm an idiot," Madison said simply.

"What are you talking about?" Aimee asked, looking concerned.

"It's about Josh. I'm an idiot. He never liked me. He never even thought about me like that," Madison confessed.

"Wait—you said he—but—I thought you said—"

"Ignore everything I said," Madison said. "I was wrong. Josh doesn't like me. He already has a girlfriend. Lindsay told me she hadn't seen him with any girls at school, but I saw him. Last night at Freeze Palace. He was with this girl Remy. Do you know her?"

"Remy McEvoy?" Aimee asked.

174

"I don't know her last name. How many Remys can there be in the ninth grade, though?" Madison said.

Brrrrrrrrring.

They tried to finish the conversation as they walked along to the next class.

"So that's it? That's the end of Josh?" Aimee asked. She sounded disappointed. "I was getting excited about the prospect of your dating some ninth grader. And then maybe you'd introduce me to some other ninth grader. . . ."

"Yeah, right," Madison said. But she smiled.

Aimee put her arm around Madison's shoulders. "You'll be okay, Maddie."

"I just feel so stupid."

"Don't say that!" Aimee said. "You are not stupid. You're . . . you're perfect."

"Yeah, well, whatever. We better get to class," Madison said.

Madison wanted to believe what Aimee said.

But she couldn't get Josh and his signs out of her head.

She was perfect, all right.

Perfectly *embarrassing*.

Her usual daily routine was back once Madison returned home that afternoon. Phin rushed to the door, panting. Mom was holed up inside her office, juggling the computer and phones. Working on the

175

final edit of her documentary was an all-consuming task.

Madison said hello to Phinnie and rushed upstairs with no more than a quick hello to Mom through the office door. Although she'd been determined to get well, Madison wasn't so sure anymore. The new plan: to bury herself as far down under the covers as possible and try hard to forget the last twenty-four hours.

Before she pulled the curtains closed in her bedroom, Madison glanced across the yard at Josh's window.

She half expected to see Josh and Remy staring back at her, laughing and pointing.

But no one was home next door.

Madison made a beeline for her bed.

"Maddie!"

Mom was calling upstairs to her.

"What?" Madison yelled back.

"Phone!" Mom screeched again. She was coming up the stairs.

"What?" Madison raced over to the door.

Mom stood there, portable phone in hand. "Didn't you hear the phone?" she asked. "Here. It's for you."

Madison took the phone and clicked the HOLD button.

"Hello?" Madison asked. She expected to hear Aimee's or Fiona's voice.

"Finnster?"

Madison sighed. Hart was one of the last people Madison felt like speaking to just then.

"Are you there?" Hart asked.

"Yeah," Madison said. "Are you calling about the science work again? Because I felt bad when I told you I couldn't do it. I mean, of course, you were right about me not liking my partner. . . ."

"That isn't why I'm calling," Hart said, clearing his throat.

"Oh," Madison said. "Then why are you calling?"

"How are you feeling?" Hart asked.

"I'm mostly better," Madison said. "Still have a little cough."

"That's good. Not the cough, I mean. It's good that you're mostly better," he said.

"What are you guys doing for your Web page project?" Madison asked.

"The Titanic," Hart said.

"That's deep," Madison said, making a bad joke.

Hart cracked up.

He thought that was funny?

Madison threw herself across her bed, phone in hand. Talking to Hart right now wasn't so bad after all. It was actually cheering her up a little.

"Did you do your science homework yet?" Hart asked.

"No," Madison said. "I am so behind in Mr. Danehy's class."

"Me, too," Hart said. "At least we're not as behind as Ivy Daly."

"Huh?" Madison said. She couldn't believe he'd brought up the name of the enemy.

"Ivy never does her work. She's always bugging me for help," Hart said.

"Really?" Madison asked.

"She's kind of annoying, in case you hadn't noticed."

Madison let out a huge roar of laughter. She couldn't help herself. The laughter just exploded from her.

"Are you okay?" Hart asked after a brief pause.

"Sorry," Madison said. "It's just that . . . well, I thought . . . never mind."

"Look, the reason I called is actually . . ." his voice trailed off.

Madison chewed on her fingernail. She needed to paint her nails. That would make her feel better, wouldn't it?

"I called because a bunch of us are going over to the Far Hill Shoppes on Saturday. And I know Egg is going to go with Fiona,"

"Yeah?" Madison said, still looking at her nails.

"Well, everyone wanted to go to the movies. . . ." Hart said.

"Uh-huh."

"And I was wondering if maybe . . . Finnster, would you go with me?"

Madison swallowed hard. She wanted to ask

178

Hart to repeat what he had just said, but she couldn't bring herself to say the words.

Had Hart Jones just asked Madison Finn out on a date?

After the embarrassment with Josh, Madison didn't know what to think. Was this some kind of practical joke masterminded by Egg? Was this another of Madison's romantic misunderstandings?

"You want me to go to the movies with you?" Madison asked.

"Exactly," Hart said, his voice perking up. "We'll all be there as a group, but everyone sort of goes as a couple—with someone else, you know?"

"Cool," Madison said.

"So, we can go together, then?" Hart asked a second time. "I'd really like that."

Madison realized that this was no misunderstanding.

"Yes!" she blurted out, not thinking anymore about it.

"Cool," Hart said. "So, tomorrow at school I'll tell you where we'll be meeting, okay?"

"Okay," Madison said. As usual, shock had her speaking in one-syllable words.

She hung up the phone.

"Rorwowowowwowowooo!" Phinnie howled and hopped up onto the bed next to Madison.

"Phin, what just happened?" Madison asked.

179

Phin cocked his head and made a whimpering noise, as if to say, "I have no idea, and why are you asking me anyway? I'm a dog!"

Madison felt tightness in the center of her belly. She had to speak to her BFFs. She had to speak to them right then and there.

Madison went online. Unbelievably, no one from her buddy list was online, so she reached for the phone again.

Aimee was at dance class.

Fiona was asleep and could not be disturbed, according to her mom.

Lindsay wasn't home yet.

Madison sent all three of them a quick, emergency e-mail. She hoped they would respond soon. Madison was ready to burst with her news.

```
From: MadFinn
To: Wetwinz; Balletgrl; LuvNstuff
Subject: CALL ME ASAP!!!
Date: Thurs 2 Oct 3:09 PM
I just got asked out on a REAL
DATE.

Call me or E me right away to find
out who asked.

xoxo Maddie

p.s.: Yes, you know him.
```

Madison got up and looked out her window again. Josh's curtains were still pulled shut, but it didn't bother Madison anymore.

She'd wanted Josh to like her so much. But maybe liking Josh was just some real-life optical illusion?

After all, Madison had wanted Hart to like her for much longer.

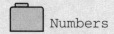 Numbers

This week when I was sick I thought a lot about numbers. You can see your whole world in numbers. For starters, I am living proof that 1 is totally the loneliest number. Even though I'm an only child I don't like being alone that much. Thanks to Phinnie, I'm not.

Gramma and I talked about numbers. We said how 2 was company but 3 was a crowd. I believe that's true 100%. When it was just 2 of us in the house it was sooooo much mellower than when it was Mom, me, and Gramma together.

I also believe that good things come in threes. Like this week I have 3 BFFS. We did great with our Web page! And that's a good thing.

But all my thoughts about numbers and my theories on Josh liking me (and not liking me) didn't prepare me for what just happened with Hart.

Rude Awakening: I may use numbers to figure out my life, but it doesn't mean that everything will add up.

Madison checked back in her e-mailbox to see if any of her BFFs had responded to her note, but the mailbox was still empty. No one had Insta-Messaged Madison, either.

She would have to wait a little longer to share the news about Hart.

But it was worth the wait.

So was he.

Mad Chat Words:

:~(~~	Poor you!
: ")	I'm so embarrassed
RN	Right now
CTS	Change the subject
AU	As usual
IKIK	I know, I know
yawn	How boring
wink	With a wink
w8!	Wait!
VVS	Very, very soon
SW?	So what?
*^_^*	Dazzling grin
TGFT	Thank goodness for that
DW	Don't worry

Madison's Computer Tip

There is nothing worse than being sick and isolated from the world. Thank goodness for my laptop. **Use e-mail to keep in touch with friends and family when you're stuck at home.** I got bronchitis but it didn't keep me from staying connected with Aimee, Fiona, and Lindsay. Best of all, Lindsay was able to use e-mail from the media lab in the library at school to keep me posted on FHJH gossip. Insta-Messages and e-mail are the best way to stay connected—without the risk of passing your cold and flu germs to your friends. Even better, I stayed in touch without anyone having to see me with my Rudolph red nose and in my wrinkled pajamas. I stayed on top of all the gossip—even the stuff about *me*!

Visit Madison at www.madisonfinn.com

Laura Dower is the author of more than sixty books for kids. Like Madison Finn, Laura is an only child, enjoys her laptop computer, and drinks root beer. She lives in New York with her husband and two children.

For updates on Madison Finn and more information about the author, log on to www.lauradower.com